T0129108

YOU AND I AM

Dr. Hyacinth B. Hue

authorHOUSE®

AuthorHouse™
1663 Liberty Drive
Bloomington, IN 47403
www.authorhouse.com
Phone: 1 (800) 839-8640

© 2017 Dr. Hyacinth B. Hue. All rights reserved.

No part of this book may be reproduced, stored in a retrieval system, or transmitted by any means without the written permission of the author.

Published by AuthorHouse 06/21/2017

ISBN: 978-1-5246-9153-0 (sc)
ISBN: 978-1-5246-9151-6 (hc)
ISBN: 978-1-5246-9152-3 (e)

Library of Congress Control Number: 2017907923

Print information available on the last page.

Any people depicted in stock imagery provided by Thinkstock are models, and such images are being used for illustrative purposes only. Certain stock imagery © Thinkstock.

This book is printed on acid-free paper.

Because of the dynamic nature of the Internet, any web addresses or links contained in this book may have changed since publication and may no longer be valid. The views expressed in this work are solely those of the author and do not necessarily reflect the views of the publisher, and the publisher hereby disclaims any responsibility for them.

Scripture quotations marked KJV are from the Holy Bible, King James Version (Authorized Version). First published in 1611. Quoted from the KJV Classic Reference Bible, Copyright © 1983 by The Zondervan Corporation.

Scripture quotations marked NIV are taken from the Holy Bible, New International Version®. NIV®. Copyright © 1973, 1978, 1984 by International Bible Society. Used by permission of Zondervan. All rights reserved. [Biblica]

Scripture quotations marked NKJV are taken from the New King James Version. Copyright © 1982 by Thomas Nelson, Inc. Used by permission. All rights reserved.

FOREWORD

The inspirational writing of ***You and I Am***, by Dr. Hyacinth B. Hue, stems from the birth and ensuing months of life of her granddaughter, Harper Camille Routliffe-Hue, born October 23, 2009. During the Christmas season at 2-months old, Harper was staging a return to her Heavenly Father's Arms due to a serious heart defect unknown to her parents and physicians.

YOU and I AM is an outstretch of the love, relationship and journey Dr. Hue desires and continues to progress toward with I AM (Father, Son and Holy Spirt) from youth to her golden years – she's 82. This book exemplifies the relationship and journey YOU can have with I AM. The story depicts the life journey of YOU and how the Great I AM knows, sees, listens, understands and participates in all matters especially the desires of your heart -- and He too desires to relate and walk on the destination with YOU to a happy, full and complete life.

I AM, who first loved Harper, heard the thoughts and prayers of many which resulted in her healing on November 3, 2010 by the gifted hands of her pediatric surgeon and the arms of love, care and protection by her first-time parents, Audrey and Herve Hue.

The journey with YOU and I AM continues whether you understand or not.

I'm honored to prepare the Foreword for Dr. Hue, whom in His Wisdom, God chose to be my mother, teacher, mentor, closest friend, wise counsel and deepest confidante. Dr. Hue is a prayer warrior for her husband, 8 children, 29 grandchildren, 7 great grandchildren, extended family and those who cross her path. Her prayer is perfume to I AM and I believe touches His "Heart". It's not by chance that I'm writing the Foreword to her 5th book on June 17, 2017. He knew that You and I AM would provide courage, faith and hope needed at this time as my husband,

Mike, of 32 years, is facing open-heart surgery on June 27th just as Harper did 7 years ago. I know my mother is praying for Mike and YOU hoping this book will touch lives so we all end up with Him.

It's a blessing to be able to share all matters of the heart with a mother expecting the truth, love, support, wisdom and PRAYER as a result of a lifetime career pursuing excellence, developing her obedience and personal relationship to our Triune God. Even better yet, we agree that I AM can be mother, father, friend, counselor and more to YOU if you allow it.

We thank God for His Love, Grace, Mercy and Healing for Harper, Mike and YOU.

Dr. Hue dedicates this book to her pediatrician, Kenneth Burk MD (Riverdale, NY), her OBGYNs Martin Kurman MD and Howard Burke, MD (Beth Israel Hospital, Manhattan, NY); Harper's heart surgeon, Samuel Weinstein MD (The Children's Hospital at Montefiore, NY); and Mike's heart surgeon, Raymond L. Singer, MD (Lehigh Valley Health Network, Allentown, PA). I dedicate this Foreword to my Dad, Eric C. Hue, Sr., a loving lifelong committed husband and father to my mother and his children. **C. Andrea Hue Gadd**

The Story of You

The Story of You is a true experience of a young infant now seven years old. The rest of the story is fiction although many events are true. The doctor in the fiction is our way of giving credit to my Jewish obstetrician that delivered most of my eight children.

The animals are based upon darling pets the children have raised and on those that my family owned when I was but a child myself.

Organization and sites relate to true experiences, admiration and respect for the wonderful word that these non-profit organizations accomplish eg. YWAM. Indeed one of these organizations is operated by the writer. These are intertwined to give a spin of hope and respect for the way God has used these programs to bless His people, especially young aspirants.

All of us is YOU. It is not difficult to live a holy life of obedience. It is definitely a choice.

Many of us delay to make the choice with accompanying consequences. We are all overcomers through Christ. Walk with YOU and let her life be an encouragement to you.

Study: The Thirteen References on Works

YOU'S SCRIPTURE ON WORKS

1. I Thessalonians 1:3

   Remembering without ceasing you work of faith, labour of love, and patience of hope in our Lord Jesus Christ in the sight of our God and Father,

2. II Thessalonians 3:10

   For even when we were with you, we commanded you this; if anyone will not work, neither shall he eat,

3. III Thessalonians 3:11

   For we hear that there are some who walk among you in a disorderly manner, not working at all, but are busybodies,

4. Titus 3:1

   Remind them to be subject to rules and authorities, to obey, to be ready for every good work,

5. Corinthians 3:13

Each one's work will become manifest; for the Day will declare it, because it will be revealed by fire; and the fire will test each one's work, of what sort it is,

6. Ephesians 4:11-12

    11. And He Himself gave some to be apostles, some prophets, some evangelists, and some pastors and teachers,

    12. for the equipping of the saints for the work of ministry, for the edifying of the body of Christ,

7. Phillipians 1:6

    Being confident that this very thing that He who has begun a good work in you will complete it until the day of Jesus Christ,

8. Collossians 1:10

    that you may walk worthy of the Lord, fully pleasing Him, being fruitful in every good work and increasing in the knowledge of God.

9. 1 Timothy 3:1

    This is a faithful saying; if any man desires the position of a Bishop, he desires a good work,

10. Hebrews 6:10

    For God is not unjust to forget your work and labour of love which you have shown toward His name, in that you have ministered to the saints, and do minister.

11. Hebrews 13:20-21

20 Now may the God of Peace who brought up our Lord Jesus from the dead, that great Shepherd of the sheep, through the blood of the everlasting covenant

21 make you complete in every good work to do His will, working in you, what is well pleasing in His sight through Jesus Christ, to whom be glory for ever and ever; Amen.

12. James 2:26

For as the Body without the Spirit is dead, so Faith without Works is dead also,

13. Revelation 2:26

And he who overcomes, and keeps My works until the end, to him I will give power over nations

Study, evaluate, meditate and learn from these Holy Scripture verses, the truth of works. You are encouraged to read all of the passages not just the verses.

INTRODUCTION

My name is **YOU** and **I AM** is my Father. YOU is a unique individual. YOU is fearfully and wonderfully made. YOU has been given the approbation to break the Queen's English, by using a singular verb. However, you may place your name or pronoun here, in place of YOU and adhere to the pureness of the English language with a verb in the plural form.

There was a season before **time** when nothing was in the universe. Void covered the deep. Then, I AM threw the world into space and emblazoned the heavens with multitudes of galaxies, stars, moon and the sun. The stars and the moon resplendent of soft, serene, quiet iridescent lights of diamonds shone at night. The moonbeams mystified the night with an eerie sense of love and devotion that would at times be worshipped as if it were its own god.

As quietly and as serendipitously as the moon retreated from its sphere the sun appeared in golden brilliance to enjoy its reign in the light of the solar system over planet earth. So too would the sun be worshipped as a god.

I AM now ordered earth to be adorned with multifaceted variety of trees, herbs, flowers, plants, fruit-bearing trees and vegetation of perfect life and form.

Living moving breathing things, animals, birds, creatures great and small were created for I AM's pleasure. They were enormous in size, yet comparisoned by a miniature of every kind. They were dressed in skins, feathers, scales, hair of every hue, every texture, all in resplendent beauty in the light of the heavens, but greater yet from the Light of I AM.

I AM created humans to dwell in the planet called earth and covenanted marriage for male and female inhabitants and rulers of the land.

Ere, the earth was thrown into space, and ere the planets were so wonderfully evolved by Creation, **I AM** knew **YOU** and called **YOU** by name.

YOU is now to be birthed in the twentieth century and in the womb of the mother. I AM placed a fertilized seed that He has now called forth from Eternity, predestined for Heaven, justified, and glorified to Eternity.

YOU will begin to germinate and grow into an image of I AM, with all the deoxyribonucleic acid (DNA) storing the genetic information of the Creator and invested in the maternal and in the fraternal parents.

The life begins as a seed (a bean) into a shape that looks like a tadpole. Magically and mysteriously juttings begin to appear. They grow into limbs that are like those of a tree, only to be budded with fingers, toes, a head with the appearances of an eye, then a face. The human being in its complexity and wonderment is becoming a child of I AM.

The flowering season of YOU's mother ceased and gestation begun. Mother began to seek the physician that would best represent the care and delivery of YOU. His obstetric training and bedside manner must be expressive of His love for infants instinctive, his tenderness towards life and fragility of an infant must be exhibited in the warmth of his handshake at his first introduction into their lives. He will also be chosen by his love for life and must be a defender of life, because a new life will be placed in his hands to succour from the first state of gestation. No matter what complication or challenge occurs, life must be his motto for YOU.

In the heavens, the Zodiacs aligned themselves in competition with great anticipation and expectation for the day of Thanksgiving for YOU. Each one desired the predestined child to be born under its reign. One Zodiac would be chosen but neither had a fore knowledge of the time, for I AM had not disclosed his plan to anyone, but to the saints of Heaven.

Special angels were assigned for the guardianship of You lest at anytime she would be in danger or even in the future dash her foot against a stone. As an infant YOU would be able to see and sense the presence of her guardian and depending on her choice of worship to and for I AM, this blessing could continue through her earthly journey.

A German Shepherd pup would be selected at the time of her birth to be a companion for You, as would also be chosen a ring-tailed Siamese cat, a lamb, a goat, a horse, a peacock and peahen.

Finally a room must be readied for YOU's arrival from the hospital of choice, St. Mary's Hospital. Until then a prayer of Thanksgiving for a life that has begun must be given and ever be given for this gift from I AM.

In holy adoration the parents kneel by their bedside and offered praise and thanks to I AM for the gift of life that they have begun to share. The Spirit of I AM descended upon them as in tears of joy they sung the Hallelujah Anthem of Handel's Messiah to HIM alone who is worthy to receive honour and praise and glory forever and ever.

The Great Preparation

Let us with a joyful mind praise I AM for HE is kind and HIS mercies endureth forever and ever, ever faithful ever sure.

The moon announces the birth of animals and man. As its golden rays shine upon the earth the waters are pulled towards the heavens. Hence we see the oceans, seas and rivers rise as if ascending to the heavens in answer to a magnetic call from a phenomenon called the moon.

Soon and very soon this moon will be awakening and pulling the waters of the amniotic sack, hastening the call to life, the infant named YOU.

Mom and Dad knew their calling was to be parents, mother and father to the children that I AM would be lending to their care. "Preparation must be made", they shared and thought. They thought of a room for the infant intrauterine and post delivery, education for the infant, religious and secular, and most of all for a manual on human development and care.

They were always mindful of the spirit of I AM in their lives and had installed a prayer closet in which to enter, pray and offer praises to God. Dad had vowed that he and his house would serve the **I AM that I AM,** unreservedly Mom in her contract of matrimony, had signed this codicil into their marriage contract. Having experienced the superb love and faithfulness of I AM through their years of preparation for priesthood and life in general, they knew without a doubt that there was no other way to raise YOU without the divine assistance of I AM.

They entered the sanctity of the prayer closet, praising I AM for HIS love and blessings, especially for this seed that was now germinating in the womb of mother. They prayed asking God for some type of instruction or manual for training YOU, whom I AM had called to be theirs. The Spirit of I AM spoke to them in an instant saying "You have a manual."

They asked, "where and what is it I AM." I AM replied, **"The word of God!"**

"The Holy Book, the Bible," they enquired. "Amen and Amen" said the great I AM.

"Wow! How could we have missed that? Of course this is the manual on which we were raised and this is the book of teaching. This is the very book of the WORD that became flesh and dwelt among us. How could we have been so blind? Eyes they have and they see not, ears they have and they hear not, until the Holy Spirit of I AM reveals it to them and to YOU.

They made a determined effort to the follow I AM's manual in its entirety, or as much as is physically and humanly possible.

They opened the Manual at this point to see what it had to say. It opened immediately and seemingly miraculously to the words: **"Train up a child** in the way he should go and when he is old, he will not depart from it."

The Word was divinely sent and in their hearts they now knew that their faith in I AM had multiplied and that the manual was **HIS Word.**

The couple thanked I AM for HIS answer to their prayer and asked for HIS direction in every process of preparation for YOU. They closed the closet door knowing that the Purpose of I AM will be fulfilled in YOU.

Now is the time to move on in finding an obstetrician for the physical and medical care of the child that is in me. I am now a mother she thought the child is in me. I am not a mother when YOU is born, but now. The Chinese date the birth of the newborn as being one year old at birth. They have that right. Life begins at conception, not at birth. You is a living being. She began to live before the foundation of the world. Both parents breathed a sigh of relief. On to the next step as we prepare for YOU.

Mother and Father Seek a Physician

After searching the Internet for the selection of the best physicians in obstetrics and paediatric care and before selecting the doctors of their choice, they met with the pastor of their Church. The Pastor ran the list through the Church's approved practising physicians to ensure that neither of them participated in abortion, which is always illegal. The word simply states, "Thou shalt not kill, no exceptions given.

The story of Solomon and the two mothers came to mind. Solomon wanting to prove the true mother, offered to divide the child in two.

The true mother asked for the child's life to be spared and given to the other woman. Solomon in his wisdom gave the child to the mother who appealed for life.

Their Pastor and the prayer group prayed with the couple and three doctors were selected at the unction of the Spirit of I AM. One doctor, and obstetrician for mother and the delivery of YOU, one a paediatrician for YOU and finally one for the mother of YOU, a gynaecologist. All would be overseen by the Great Physician, I AM.

Appointments were made for obstetric care, month by month, until the eighth and ninth months when they were checked every two weeks.

The first visit incorporated dietary recalls and regimen, blood work, physical exercises and a schedule for ultrasound. All was well. Each month's visit brought the same result of perfect development; heart beat blood pressures, and blood counts. The mother suffered no excessive nauseas, bingeing nor cravings. Her diet was nutritionally sound. If at no other time in her life she wanted things to be right, this was the time. She stayed away from alcohol, except for the Eucharist and wine. She ingested no medication for pain or for any other reason. She abstained from anything that would be a contraindication to the health of this precious child.

Every meal was devotedly blessed, every act presented to I AM for confession, forgiveness and direction. The house was full of joy and gladness as each day they entered His courts with praise?

Preparation of YOU's Nursery

Having ensured that the health of YOU, and her mother was optimum, it was time for a nursery to be prepared for her homecoming from the hospital. This is the place where she would receive the warmth of love in a home, the comfort of her new environment and the tender nurturing that would be as the DNA of her spiritual and social formation.

The guardian angels assigned to YOU were busily preparing the nursery for a sanctuary of home, faith and love for YOU and her parents.

Heavenly tunes could be heard as silence permeated the dwelling, especially when the couple prayed or were asleep.

The angels stood guard when necessary and encouraged the nestlings that had taken abode in the lilac tree beneath the window of the room. The cardinal would solo or join with the angels in chorister's songs of love and praise. I AM said, "This is good." The angels commuted between YOU's abode and heaven as they reported to God the blessings that transpired in this spiritual abode called **home.**

In this house is unity. This house will stand. It is not divided against itself. Oh what blessedness! Oh what hope is YOU. She is standing on the promises of I AM.

CHAPTER 1

YOU IS BORN

YOU's Homecoming

Birth is like death and death like birth. Birth is leaving the heavenly home and arriving in a new planet, not before known. The shock must be severe as we hear the infant scream.

Death is birth into a new realm, entirely different from planet earth. Similar, but pure and resplendent of the beauty and glory if I AM.

When a child arrives, he has no inkling of the place she has arrived, and the citizen of earth upon departure has no knowledge of where he is going, so death offers a scare. The infant is received with love and hospitality and the same is true when a saint arrives. The arms of Abraham's bosom receive him with much greater love and hospitality than any human can offer.

Both have fear and trepidation, which immediately vanish in the atmosphere of unadulterated and unconditional love. You have no fear of birth and will have no fear of "death". What we call death and the end is just the beginning – of eternal life.

The final trimester of gestation was almost completed. Back pains begun to bear down on the mother, as the pressure on the uterus intimidated her walk. She could no longer skip and bend. The judgement of the sorrow of labour was upon her, but this was only the beginning. The pain of labour would soon be forgotten.

A tidal wave developed in the uterus. YOU somersaulted into a reverse position, head towards the exit door.

The door begun to open a centimetre at a time, but only the strength of YOU could totally open the door of the birthing canal.

Would she have the strength? The force would be ingratiating to mother, but love suffers long and is kind.

The moon was in its fullest light, round and yellow with the gold of love and light. It's mystified force attracted the waters of planet earth and mystified the water of the womb, seated in the embryonic sack. The water begun to move as if it were at boiling temperature. The force ruptured the sack as water flowed downwards to the feet of Mother. This magnetism invigorated YOU as she started her push to force the door open. A spot of blood showed and the call was made for the luggage that had been packed for the hospital. All three sped away in the family car, their goal the delivery room of the hospital.

The Nursery for YOU

This room was spacious, painted in light pink, with streams of white paint edging the mid-walls like ribbons. The room felt like peaches and ice cream, and the smell as fresh as roses.

On a small shelf under the window rested a cherubic icon of the nativity. The holy family seemed to be anticipating the new arrival. The brush of angel wings could be felt as they ministered their angelic performance.

The cradle was hand made by Father, and dressed in white skirts, pink coverlets and blanket. The pillows were embroidered in pictures of daisies, and forget-me-nots festooned with green vines.

A rocking chair with a large Teddy bear sat by the window. Mobiles decorated the entire room and they danced in circles as if propelled by the music of the angels.

A dresser with a mirror, painted the purest white, as was the cradle, held neatly folded clothing, toiletry, cotton balls and buds, sterilization equipment and other needed articles.

A top the dresser was a framed picture of the ultrasound image of YOU. Next to this was a picture of the Holy Family and one of the mother and father of YOU. YOU's first picture would soon be added, as would YOU and her later pictures. The room would soon be reverberating with life.

The Hospital

In the Girl's Scout and Boy's Scout both mother and dad in their youth, learned to "be prepared". They took every precaution to be ready for this moment.

Pre registration was made at the hospital. The obstetrician was called the moment her water broke and he gave instruction for them to meet him at the hospital. He had just finished his supper when Father called. He was free to fulfil his commitment to deliver YOU and to present YOU to her mother's waiting arms.

He got ready, entered his car and was on his way to the hospital feeling satisfied after a delicious meal, and a lovely conversation with his family. They prayed over supper and asked God's blessing on any emergency call that came in, because tonight he was on "call" at the hospital. Although a private physician, he gave time to the hospital in preparation of God's blessing on his life and on his family's.

Medical school had been a challenge, his mother passed while he was in high school. She was giving birth to a boy that would be his brother. The shock set his father back for a while, but eventually they overcame the shock and with the help of I AM, their life without a wife and mother was back on track. The challenge of medical school was almost overwhelming, but as a student in medical school, he forged his way promising himself that by the help of I AM, he would complete his purpose. His purpose was to be the best in obstetrics so that the careless mistake that took his mother's life would never happen again. His fight was in research of techniques that could save lives at birth and to ask I AM's help in assuring that no life (mother or child) would be lost under his medical supervision and assistance.

God answered his prayers.

He drove cautiously yet hurriedly. He whispered a prayer of thanks to I AM for keeping all the promises He gave. So far he lost no one. His record was unbelievable. Three thousand births, no loss of parent or infant. I AM is faithful and just to forgive all our sins and to cleanse us from all unrighteousness. Truly, I have been sinful. I blamed God for my mother's death. Dad drank for a while until the love of the Church and their prayers brought him back into fellowship. "I have a lot to be grateful for." He prayed as he turned his eyes up to heaven as if he saw into Heaven where I AM was seated.

He had a blessed assurance that all would go well tonight. He was at the hospital before he knew it. He parked his car and headed to the delivery area of the hospital. He arrived at the labour room simultaneously as mother.

Mother was in the labour room strapped to the gurney. She was panting hard. The pain in her low back was excruciating. The labour pains got sharper and sharper. She felt as if a tornado was getting ready to blow and there was no space for this to happen. You felt as if she were trapped in hell or death. She had to fight hard to get out of this place that once was so comfortable and safe, but now gave her eviction notice.

She pushed her head downwards as if she were diving into something solid. Something like a large rose appeared over her head. The petals burst open and liquefied as blood, it covered her face and body. Earlier she felt as if she were being moved with her mother and truly she was. She was now with her mother in the delivery room.

Her mother thought of the curse of woman "in pain will you bring forth children."

She gave herself in resignedly to her fate and pushed. You felt the energy of her mother and joined in as the door immediately opened and YOU floated into the hands of Dr. Kurman. He held her by her legs and gave a gently slap on the tiny buttocks. Air pumped into her seemingly aquatic being and the voice box or larynx exploded with a tiny scream. YOU is now in a new world. She has been called forth by I AM. She is being washed and wrapped in swaddling cloth and placed into the arms of her waiting mother.

She has been waiting for nine months for this moment. Her father's hand bore the bruises of the hold on his hand by Mother. He tried to shake off the pain as he reached for this new part of his life, his being. Together, they held her safe and tenderly sharing arms of love as they experienced a calm and peace that seemed unnatural. Yes, truly unnatural. It was supernatural.

God called forth from before time a child to be born in our time; a girl as pink as the delicate petals of a rose. Under the translucent veil called skin, shone blue and red arteries and veins like a road map. The pink flesh beneath would soon be colourings and pigments of the skin. For now she was a rose of variegated colours or shapes of pink and red.

All infants are born with pink or red skin. The tip of the ears and the fingers beneath the nail could alert you of the true colours.

YOU is checked for fingers and toes. All are accounted for. The nails are soft and tender. Her fingers show slimness and were extraordinary lengthy, the sign of a true musician and pianist, maybe.

Her hair is light and feathery with a light brown tinge to it. Her brows are of the same shade of brown matching long curvaceous lashes. Her eyes are like diamonds reflecting the inner being of her soul. She is not yet able to focus on the light, but her eyes are clear and bright. No jaundice here.

Her stomach is good, breast good, reflex good, strength of fingers good. She is holding the forefinger of her father. Love was flowing from one to the other. The thrill of love between father and YOU was ecstatic. They are not yet bonded yet the flow of love was unstoppable. He would die to protect the life of YOU.

No greater love has any man for this child. He came back to reality. The thought of him fighting for YOU's life started an adrenalin rush. He was breathing heavily. He spoke a quiet prayer of thanks and asked I AM's protection for them all.

In all the excitement no one gave YOU any sustenance. This was brought to focus almost two hours after birth. Mother attempted to give her natural milk. Goat gives their kids goat's milk. Cows give their calves cow's milk, cat, cat's milk and so on.

It did not seem natural that you could not receive the milk. The grandmother, acted like the proverbial fly on the wall. She felt that the denial of sucrose or glucose at birth had weakened the ability of her grandchild to suck and release the flow of milk. She said nothing. There are times in the life of man, that family become invisible. The focus is so personal at times that any loved one seems to be an intruder. This was one of these times. The focus was first mother; then mother and YOU; then father, mother, YOU and the medical team. The relatives that ran to the house and to the hospital are often not remembered until the nurse comes out and announces, "It's a girl (or boy)!"

They may be subconsciously, unremembered, but they always remember. Go to the hospital Chapel, they are there. Go to the homes, look in the bedroom or the bathroom, there they are on their knees interceding to I AM on behalf of their loved ones and their condition.

As one ages and as he grows spiritually in faith he realizes that in these circumstances he/she should stand still and see the salvation of I AM. That does not mean he should stand by and do nothing, or say nothing. Stand in faith and pray and having done all, stand.

After the cleansing of the infant, YOU, she was wheeled in a basinet to the nursery while mother was taken to her assigned room for a rest that was so needed after the breathtaking ordeal. The young YOU was later brought in and each visitor had the opportunity to peak at her, or to hold her for a moment.

The sweet aromatic oil of anointing that permeates a newborn is irresistible. No one to our knowledge can resist the temptation to snuggle his/her nose to the neck of the child and inhale the purity of love and holiness. YOU's oil perfumed her blanket and clothing. Her body sprayed the room with this sweet anointing. Is it any wonder that everyone wanted to hold her to his breast even for a moment?

Pictures were being taken of YOU and her parents. Everyone wanted a first day picture of this blessed infant. She was so beautiful and wonderfully made. These pictures were later shared personally, on the internet, telephone and via the U.S. mail. All were delighted to hold this lovely creature in their hands, even if it were just a picture. A picture speaks louder than a thousand words. She would be prominently displayed in every home and office. Equal numbers of prayers were being said on behalf of YOU and her family.

Angels were appearing in the hospital and before the face of I AM, carrying the good news of YOU's birth and the prayer team that never ceased to pray and to give thanks to I AM.

In due time, YOU was checked out of the hospital and was safely in her cradle in her nursery. Mother and father could not wait to be in their home where 'prayer' was the watchword and where the sanctity of the house gave way to unbridled praise and thanksgiving.

CHAPTER 2

A HOME FOR YOU

The Permanent Abode

A man seeks a permanent place to reside, grow and enjoy the last years of his life. One should ask and answer the question if there is any permanence on earth. The answer is that maybe, that for as long as we live, this is permanent. On the other hand this may be our temporary home.

Looking at the splendour of the land, its landscape, the pets on the form and at the lovely home, mother and father anticipated this unique and blessed setting a permanent abode for YOU. This blessing that arrived a few days ago, should enjoy a hope for life, if God wills it to be so.

Should YOU have the desire to choose, she should not have asked for anything more.

I AM divinely inspired and directed mother and father in the preparation and reception for YOU. Even the weather was perfect for her homecoming.

The nurse wheeled mother to the waiting car after placing YOU into father's arms. He walked militantly close to the wheelchair, as if to protect both of his wards at the same time. His eyes flashed from side to side as if aware of some unforeseen danger. They arrived safely to the car. The rear door opened and on the seat was a child's car seat strapped securely on the right passenger seat. The nurse placed and strapped in the car seat the sleeping YOU, as mother slid in next to her.

Father was to chauffeur all the way home as the humming sounds of the automobile lulled YOU deeper into sleep.

The only conversation between the driver and the adult rider was on the blessing that I AM brought to them. They prayed a short prayer of thanks before the journey began and the conversation was a repetition of the content of the prayer.

In a short time they were parked at the driveway by the door of their home and the door opened by the proud chauffeur and father to exist mother. He then unshackled the infant and walked to the door. Mother tried to collect the luggage, but he sweetly told her to let it be, for he would be back to retrieve it after they were safely landed in their comfortable quarters.

Mother felt very uncomfortable that she was not allowed to hold YOU in her arms on the way home. She begrudged the car seat and wished there was never that law. Resignedly, she gave in to her thoughts realizing that this law was in place for the safety of YOU, just as the seat belt law protected her and father from past danger.

As I AM serving-Christians, they must observe these laws of man, so that they would be able to obey the laws of I AM whom they could not see. Which of these is easier, they mused?

The Manual on "Raising You" would be immediately brought to the forefront, to be checked regularly for the rules and regulation on "Bringing Up YOU". This same Manual brought up father and mother and many before them. There was no resistance to this act; without the **word** they would not be the people they are today.

As a matter of fact, YOU would not be there. For a genetic fault in mother's inherited trait warned of difficulty in the birth of their children. They had been advised not to have children and to abort if pregnancy developed. This is one of the reasons for their faith in I AM and for their faith against abortion. Their motto: "Trust in I AM with all Thine Heart and lean not unto thine own understanding." They refused to lean unto their own understanding. I AM would and should always direct their path!

Mother was served a refreshing snack and ordered to rest while YOU rested. Nights could grow long and the days testy. "Rest while it is day." The Manual is officially launched!

The telephones are ringing off the hooks. The door bell rings and rings. The father thinks of detaching the ring-tone, while mother wishes she could disconnect the telephone. Better judgement prevails. The phone is our outside link and our prayer link. Visitors are an asset. They bring a meal. They hold YOU so the parents can get a needed break. They encourage and pray with the family. They run short errands. They even help in cleaning. They bear one another's burden.

Giving birth to a child is taxing, nerve racking, costly and at times cause depression post-partum. Family and friends never get weary of doing good. The couple learned a long time ago that they should be willing to receive, as they were willing to give. Unless they received, how could their family and friends be blessed in giving? Receiving is a gift. Giving is a blessing. Both are from I AM.

Wherever YOU went her guardian angels followed unseen, unfelt and undisturbed. Their mission was guarded. Visitors who were insightful, discerning and spiritually anointed and attuned felt their presence in the form of a spiritual anointing. The sign of the slightest hint of danger to YOU or to her parents would spring these worshippers into prayers of intercession, confession, forgiveness and reconciliation.

Meanwhile the angels as seen by YOU, were making more frequent trips between Heaven and Earth. Was something brewing? The brush of angel wings was now being felt, but unassigned. It was as a breath of fresh air that atomized the oils of rose and love from the anointed pores of YOU. YOU know something was awry. She moaned a lot. She spat up a lot. She gained no weight.

It was decided that it was time to call in the paediatrician before her six-weeks check-up and before her mother's appointment.

Catastrophe and YOU

Faith and love were at excelis point. Hope was at its optimum point in the house. Trust was ultimatum for the circle of friends and family in this home were all on the same plateau of friendship with I AM with whom they experienced a personal relationship.

What a fellowship, what a joy divine!

Leaning in the Everlasting Arms.

Each time YOU was fed, she regurgitated the milk. It was not the result of an allergy. There was only a four-ounce gain in weight in the period of one month of her young life. The paediatrician offered a form of medication to calm the stomach, with no responding positive result.

Christmas arrived. The problem with YOU continued. Family went to visit YOU for the season. Among them was Nanny (Grandma) whose faith was unfailing. Observing the condition of YOU, she took YOU into her arms, anointed her (with permission) sung to her and prayed over her in silence. The Spirit of I AM told Nanny that YOU would gain weight. Nanny shared the good news and continued to sing quietly in the ears of YOU.

> "Jesus loves me this I know
> For the Bible tells me so
> Little ones to him belong
> They are weak buy He is strong
>
> Cho: Yes, Jesus loves me, Yes Jesus loves me!
> Yes, Jesus loves me! The Bible tells me so.
> Jesus loves me, He will stay
> Close beside me all he way
> If I love Him when I die
> He will take me home on high
>
> Jesus loves me, He who died,
> Heaven's gate to open wide
> He will take away my sin
> Let His little child come in.

YOU cuddled closely to the voice that carried the tune. She smiled and looked around the room as if to listen to the angels that joined in. She truly enjoyed the visit and the song. She smiled over and over until the visitors departed, so that she could be 'fed' and put to rest.

On the way home a call was received informing Nanny that YOU was on her way to the hospital. The regurgitation had increased. By the next day YOU lost the one-pound she gained. This seemed the antithesis of the prophetic word that Nanny spoke. Nanny was not deterred. She spoke, "The devil is a liar."

The holidays were filled with activities as usual. There is a busyness at this time of year for everyone. The worst is that this is vacation time.

The paediatrician, fortunately, was reached. Tests showed that there was a serious problem in YOU. Why did this go undetected before and for so long? This was life-threatening if not dealt with immediately or very soon. Blame was bounced around for a while and discarded into the basket of unworthiness and unrighteousness.

Prayer chains were opened. The telephone in heaven began to ring. Sweet perfume surrounded the nostrils of I AM as the prayers of the saints encircled the Throne. Angels were ministering to YOU and to the saints with lightening speed. They tickled YOU and kept her smiling and looking for her dad, each time he moved from her sight to cry out to God and to tear.

Doctors from out of town offered to send their team to work on YOU, if the paediatric cardiologist could not return from his vacation on time. The surgical team would accompany the surgeon to work in place of the vacationing staff/team.

The paediatric surgeon on vacation was reached. He decided that the surgery could wait for the New Year. He was the best in the region.

In a day the Nanny was back at the hospital. She kept a free watch on the events after taking a peak at YOU and blessing her with the oil of anointing.

She spent all day investigating procedures and found a mother whose son suffered from the same medical problem as YOU. She prayed with the mother for complete healing after being told that her son had a successful surgery the month before. This news encouraged the faith of YOU's parents. Surgery was scheduled for the first week of the New Year and Nanny returned home to await the good news, after a prayer of praise and thanksgiving to I AM for his continued mercy and grace. She was on her way over the Verezano Narrows Bridge when an anxious call was received. The bad news was that the pressure from YOU's heart, after her being fed, pressed against her lung and the lung collapsed.

Nanny began to pray all over again. She thanked I AM that YOU would gain weight and asked Him to inflate YOU's lung. I AM spoke to her and said, "She has two lungs". Nanny gave a weird shout of thanks, subdued by laughter as she exclaimed, "That's why you gave us two lungs. If one went bad, the other would function. Thanks You, I AM!

CHAPTER 3

MIRACULOUS REPAIR

The Diagnosis and Prognosis

Father and Mother were overly concerned about the situation that YOU was experiencing and reasonably so. You fought like a soldier to overcome the severe regurgitation that followed each meal. The fluid entered the chest cavity and seemed to drown her heart. After each episode, she forced a beautiful smile of encouragement towards her parents, whose tears became mixed with hope as they observed her gesture of faith and love.

Their hearts were literally breaking, for they had no understanding of what was happening to YOU. Upon arriving at the paediatrician's office, an appointment was made for emergency tests for blood work, x-rays and MRIs. This was six weeks after her six-week's check-up following her birth. The urgency seemed late, everyone thought, but better late than never. Late is bad, but now let's look towards the future, the family agreed. I AM is in charge. He is never late. 'Remember' Lazarus' death, "they sighted. He was dead, but the purpose was resurrection. Let us give thanks and be hopeful, they agreed. Out of evil comes forth good. I AM will be using this our sorrow to bring forth good.

I AM gave YOU to Father and Mother for their protection over YOU. They felt unworthy of that gift. They were not able to protect YOU. As they waited to be called for the findings on the results of these tests, their anxiety grew. Doubters shared their "feelings". The parents and grandparents rebuked the evil misgivings and encouraged one another with the truth that I AM called YOU into the world for a purpose. As a matter of fact that is the meaning of I AM. "**The I AM of purpose.**" I **AM the King of Kings.**" "**I AM the true vine.**" "**I AM the Deliverer.**" I AM whatever you have need of "Jehovah Jireh."

YOU needed I AM in every Divine Attribute of the Personification of His power and will. They prayed and confessed their sins again for the healing of YOU.

The results as related to them by the paediatrician showed that there were two holes in the little heart of YOU. One was small and could be easily fixed, but the other was larger and would be more difficult. The time to do the surgery would also prove more difficult for YOU. A time and date of the surgery was given. The surgeon was back from a well-earned vacation as were his team of surgical staff. Hearts began to beat heavily. Fear was subdued by the knowledge of the love of I AM.

The medical team left the conference room, the parents returned to the bedside of YOU in the paediatric surgical ward. The grandparents returned to their temporary abode to await the result of the surgery. They would not be at the hospital since both of the parents of YOU would be there from early morning through the length of the surgery and recovery time. They would relay all the necessary information on the prognosis as the day moved on.

Early the next morning, YOU was taken to the operating room after kissing her parents goodbye. As a matter of fact, they kissed her. She weakly followed them with her eyes as she was wheeled away and offered a faint smile. She was under the influence of the anaesthesia.

Father and mother, despite their strength and their prayer to I AM for a miraculous recovery felt their hearts being torn out of their chests, as the tears flowed involuntarily down their cheeks. They had neither the energy not the will to wipe the tears away, for they held each other's arms very tightly and they were wearied from lack of sleep. They had no sleep for many days and nights. They had not eaten for a long time. They did not remember when the last time was. Fortunately very little milk was required by YOU, so the expressed amount would suffice for now.

With great encouragement on the wisdom of rest and nutrition, they were encouraged to take both, for the wait for the procedure to be over, would be very lengthy.

They hung in close proximity to the theatre lest there were any news on need for them to be seen or called.

After what seemed like many days, they were called. The good news was that the surgery was over and that everything went well. She was being taken to the recovery room, and they were invited to meet YOU there.

YOU was beginning to awaken. Her father leaned over her as her mother leaned on his shoulders to keep from falling. YOU opened her beautiful eyes for a moment, stared at her father, smiled at him and returned to the land of sleep, where angels sang and danced in the presence of I AM, and where little children played and frolicked in joyful wonder, of the beautiful heaven of rest.

Father and mother breathed a sigh of relief and fell into a love seat near by in order to wait by her bedside with the guardian angels assigned to YOU. The angels continued their busy schedule between YOU and I AM, sharing the good news of heaven and earth. All would be well.

I AM had given wisdom and dexterity to the paediatric surgeon and the team. They had done well. They had committed their life and actions to the will of I AM. I AM was grateful for their obedience and blessed them unconditionally.

The team praised and thanked I AM for His wisdom and strength during the delicate surgery. The parents thanked I AM, the team and the doctors for their hard work of love. This was a day of thanksgiving, of praises and love. All was well in the world.

YOU told her guardian angels that she was happy and thankful to everyone, especially to I AM. She promised to be obedient, to get well, to gain weight, and to serve I AM with all her heart and with all her strength.

She pledged to listen to her parents, to be obedient to them and to fulfil the purpose for which she was called into the Earth.

She grew and slept in order to get well, promising to take nourishment that was offered so that the prophetic word as told by Nanny would be fulfilled. Nanny had faith. Everyone hoped for the best results. "Faith is the substance of things hoped for, the evidence of things not seen." YOU and her family and friends had seen the evidence. I AM is the fulfilment of all things.

YOU is discharged from the HOSPITAL

The near loss of YOU, the complexity of coping with all the issues, schedules, travelling, sleeplessness and anxiety should have weakened a giant. But, somehow the comfort and strength of I AM through HIS people in the form of family, friends and prayer partners from the global community supported and encouraged the entire family of YOU.

Very soon after the surgical operation, in an open-heart procedure, YOU began to improve. She could now digest and keep down her food. Her appetite increased and in a week she regained the pound weight that she lost at Christmas. She was now only a pound over her birth weight at three months of age.

Thankfully, her vital signs had not diminished. Her little brain seemed to be functioning appropriately as she responded to the tests performed by her Godly paediatrician. He must have had recrimination about the late identification of the birth defect, but no one mentioned that fact, and neither did he. His loyalty and service through the recuperation and continued care of YOU showed his love and support and concern and that was sufficient for all.

All rejoiced when the day and time came for YOU to be discharged from the hospital. What a joy and relief this was. It was even more exhilarating than the discharge after YOU's birth. Everyone breathed a sigh of relief and let down their proverbial hair in an attitude of peace for YOU's guardian angels seemed to be a little less active in their departure to and from the throne of I AM. Although angels show no emotion, YOU and the spiritually discerning, knew without a doubt that her angels were more on guard at her side than by moving to report to I AM as expeditiously as before.

This time she was taken to the car by the nurse who passed her to her mother who was now seated in the rear passenger seat. She carefully and tenderly strapped YOU in with soft cushions between her and the seat belt of her carrier. Mother hugged both carrier and child as father gently and carefully whizzed them away towards the sanctuary called home.

With great caution and less ado, she was taken into the nursery, car seat and all, and lovingly extricated from the constraining yet protective carrier that no one likes, but finds to be a necessary and protective commodity.

It kept YOU firm, from any bump on the road, as well as from twisting and turning with the natural curves on the driving road.

Once again she was safely in the nurture and admonition of her parents and extended family. You looked around her room, at the mobile over her cradle in which she was once again securely placed. She smiled at mother and father and finally she smiled a "thank you" to her guardians as she drifted off into a sleep that was so refreshing and restful; that after a few hours the parents thought it wise to awaken her and give her sweet nourishment and comfort, close to the bosom of her mother.

She ate with great desire and appetite as the milk flowed warmly into her mouth, down her oesophagus into her stomach. The warmth exuded to her heart and encouraged the warmth of love that was already there. It was as if the blood that had previously flowed from her heart, was now being replaced.

Somewhere in her dream or in her unconsciousness, she learned of the blood that flowed from the heart of I AM for her healing. She accepted the sacrifice. YOU felt akin to this suffering and rejoiced that she could suffer as I AM suffered for her. A kinship between Father and daughter, Saviour and friend, who were now bonded forever. Everlasting life was hers to receive and she believed.

"YOU WILL GAIN WEIGHT"

The team at home, coupled with the medical team were now philosophically married to each other for as long as she needed a paediatrician.

Together they monitored, nurtured and examined YOU on a regularly scheduled basis. She gained adequate and average weight for a child at the age of one, which she now was.

By her second birthday, she was active, alert, smart, happy and as loving any two year old could be.

Despite the set back in her ability to sit up at three month old, to crawl by six months of age, she caught up with all the measured activities that are psychologically measured for the care and development of infants and toddlers. At the age of six months she learned to wave as the Queen Mother of England did. No one taught YOU to wave good-bye or hello. It was considered that her guardians on entrance and departure (which were instantaneous) had engraved this gift into her beautiful soul. She was a princess of no mean order. I AM is King, YOU is His heir and daughter. He called her forth. She obeyed and here she was full of light and love and joy and the exact weight that she ought to be at the age of two years old.

HER GIFTS AND TALENTS

At the tender age of two years of age, she began to show special gifts and talents not usually seen in toddlers. The manifestation of the blessings became apparent soon after her baptism.

You suffered quietly during the months of recuperation and very soon after the staples from her chest were removed and healing had taken place, the church and her parents planned her Baptism or Christening, for not only was she now a part of Dr. Kurmun and his staff but the Church community became an extension of the family as well.

Her first birthday was decided as the Baptismal date. She should be dedicated to the Lord on this day as a memorial of her second birth. One may think that this is unwise, since she was not of age to accept I AM as her Saviour and Lord, but I AM had already accepted her before time begun. He restored her to good health, while sparing her life. Jesus was dedicated as an infant and so was Samuel. These examples were sufficient. Her Baptism into I AM was delayed already and now was the opportune time.

Dressed in the most charming white gown, white bonnet, white shoes and leotards she was presented to the Lord liturgically, blessed with oil and holy water poured over her head as a symbol of submersion. The moment the water was poured upon her, she raised her arms to heaven as if is praise and whispered "Aba" which everyone interpreted as Father, I AM or God. Then her right hand went up, down and from left to right as if she were blessing the family of I AM with the sign of the Cross. All were in amazement.

After Baptism she was observed in prayerful postures and genuflecting before the Creshe in her memory. Was she learning these gestures from her guardians or from Church?

Whenever mother or father was troubled or feeling ill, she groaned with each of them as each held her in his or her arms. She became sensitive to their feelings and emotions although they did not overly display them.

The cat and dog were bought and given to her when she was six months old. She played with them as siblings. They watched over her as she slept although neither of them went into her bed. When she awoke she stroked them gingerly, hugged them and crawled around the room with them. They literally taught her to crawl and by the time she was a year old at her Christening they had taught her to walk by nudging her up from the rear. They were six months her junior.

Should she attempt to get into trouble, the kitten would meow and the pup would bark. Upon hearing these sounds she would stop in her tracks or retreat from her excursion.

Her parents learned the type of sounds each pet made when trouble was brewing. The playful bark of the dog or cry from the kitten was of a completely different crescendo.

She was now in a crib and at one point she climbed up and fell out of her safe heaven. The playmates made such an uproar that mother came running to the rescue. Siddie used his body to defect he fall and ended up limping for a few days. This was breathtaking.

As soon as she could talk, she named him Laddie and the kitten Siddie. Neither of them had much hair; therefore the shedding of hair was minimal. They were properly trained. Siddie was trained to use the toilet. For a while her sand was placed in the nursery bathroom over the toilet. Once she got used to using it there, it was removed and she continued to use the same positions and to flush.

Since her room door was always kept open, Laddie had the freedom to leave, bark at the door to be let out, and to be let in as he went to the area marked for his pit stop. This area was cleaned daily and sanitized. It was also a fixed area, so that you could not enter when she became a toddler. Later a door was placed in the door, so that Laddie could let himself out freely. Siddie was not allowed outside, lest she strayed and attracted fleas or other pests and dirt.

Both animals were bathed regularly and when YOU learned to swim before she was two years old, Laddie swam with her. It was a delight to watch her and her playmates and wards.

There was no time for loneliness nor ennui for YOU had a group of friends, playmates and guardians, Laddie, Siddie and her angels.

At two years of age, she sung songs for everyone. She learned Jesus Love The Little Children, Jesus Loves Me This I Know and I Love Him. It was amusing to hear her sing as she pronounced the words, first in "Baby Language" and as she developed in speech, she sung as clearly as a bell.

It was her delight to look at the stars. Her father loved astronomy and taught her the name of the stars and the Zodiacs. Very soon she could name them as well as he.

Her interest in dinosaurs led her into the names of these prehistoric creatures and by the age of three she identified each of the species by name.

YOU was more than delighted at the sight of birds. The cardinals made the lilac bush their home before her birth. As she grew they continued to nestle there. It is said that birds nestle where there is contentment.

Mother bought her a book of birds on her first birthday. She enjoyed turning the pages with her or with father, until she was able to do so by herself. She knew the names of the birds in the book. By age four she teased her parents on their resemblance to these godly creatures.

YOU loved birds, animals and men. Her greatest past time was her weekend visits to the zoo, and to the botanical gardens.

Television did not excite her much for she seemed drawn to nature and to people.

At age five a horse was added to her family of friends. She learned to ride and could not wait for the time when she could saddle up and ride away on her own with Laddie racing along or behind. Laddie was a Rottweiler with wings of speed, a good temperament, but powerfully protective. He knew friend from foe and would offer his life to protect YOU.

The parents thought of home schooling YOU. They weighted the pros and cons and decided that the Parochial School offered all and more than they could. Two of the deciding factors were Religious Education, and Socialization. With prayer and I AM's direction they decided on the Parochial School from pre-school to high school. The decision for college could be made later and the choice would be primarily YOU's.

CHAPTER 4

MIRACLES CONTINUE

YOU'S SENSE OF RESPONSIBILITY

YOU established her interest in birds, animals, plants, the planets and prehistoric creations, as well as a sincere interest in the environment in which she lived.

Her recitation of things learned showed and intelligence far exceeding her age level. YOU memorized scripture verses, songs and ditties.

She told and retold Bible stories, parables the miracles of I AM, and the history that she created, added to those of her family. She never forgot the story of the miraculous healing of her heart and compared it to the broken and pierced heart of I AM.

No tear was ever shed in memory of the repaired holes in her heart, but many a tear was shed as she heard or spoke of the hole in the heart of I Am. His hole was placed there by a man such as YOU. This added kinship with I AM and increased her love and devotion to Him. Her prayers always included forgiveness for YOU's participation in injuring her FATHER.

She called no man henceforth father. Mother and Father were now delegated to Mary and I AM; and to her parents, Mom and Dad.

She saw her parents as a part of or an extension of the Holy Trinity and her angels. She continued to see her heavenly guardians all her earthly life. She named them Michael and Angelica. They seemed to be males but their tenderness gave them the feminine spirit of her Mom and their strength reminded her of her Dad. These similarities caused her to equally divide their oneness into male and female. She thought of Michael and Michelle, but that gave too much of a human gender.

They were angels. Michael is a great angel! Angelica means angel. That settled it. Mom and Dad agreed, and showed their admiration of her choice in names, with great big hugs and kisses.

Everyone marvelled at the wit and intelligence of this little creation of I AM. During one of these quizzical moments YOU replied, "I have the wisdom of I AM. He made me in His image." All laughed heartily and amazingly together.

At age three she made her own bed each day. She participated, in her way, in all the household activities and duties until she was able to be in total control of each tool or implement.

Her hair was manageable. YOU brushed and maintained its neatness at all times.

YOU took care of her pets, cleaning and grooming, watering and feeding. Her horse, Whiteman, she could not reach to groom for a long time; so she managed with Dad holding her within reach. She then graduated to a step stool until at the age of nine or ten she was at a height when she could reach her ride at the appropriate height. She grew to the height of five-feet nine inches. YOU considered that to be a model height for her as a girl. She was more than comfortable with her weight and height.

She maintained her own laundry and wardrobe, keeping her clothing, shoes and hats in an immaculately ordered state. One would think she was trained in the military. Although her parents were disciplinarians, many whispered that her training was the hand of her guardians, and that for a special purpose that would be forthcoming.

The greatest sense of accomplishment was her art. She drew and painted as a professional. Her framed work decorated the house. YOU entered early competitions and gained first place in state, country and internationally. She was unaffected by any of her accomplishments.

Her heart was in music and dance. YOU started dance and piano at age three. Ballerina was her favourite and she excelled in it. YOU was akin to classical music, which she played with the dexterity of a genius. It was as if she was off in a wonderland of her own.

It melted the hearts of its hearers as she played and or danced. Friends and family realized that their anxieties and stresses were removed as they listened to her play or saw her dance. Later they began to realize that healing was taking place in their bodies during these times, of what they thought entertainment. More was to come. Was this the purpose to which YOU was called? Time would tell.

YOU was filled with joy and gladness. This joy caused her to leap and to dance. It was abundant and abounding joy. This joy was an abiding joy that resided in her at all times.

This joy flowed out of her in music, dance, art and song. YOU was totally dependent upon God. The song that Nanny whispered in her ear at three months old stayed in her heart. Jesus loves me! Yes, Jesus loved me. The continuous feeding of the Word in her heart, settled in, bore fruit and resonated from her being. She was obedient to her parents and to the commandments of I AM. In order to obey I AM, YOU must first love and obey those who have the rule over her. YOU respected and obeyed her teachers, pastors, elders, music teacher, dance instructor and at sixteen and beyond her driving instructor and instructions. She wanted to live long upon this beautiful land called planet Earth. I AM made it especially for her, with all the blessings and benefits that went with it.

She prepared herself for the First Communion by reading all the information she could gather on the Eucharist. The instruction came from her pastor and parents. Several stories on the healing benefits of the Bread and Wine were shared with her. A very remarkable one was from her grandfather who was miraculously healed after partaking of the Communion Bread and Wine, (the Body and Blood) of I AM. Pop was unable to eat after colon surgery. The ingestion of the Body and Blood gave him immediate appetite and complete healing without benefit of medication or any other medical treatment. His doctor confirmed his healing without calling it a miracle, although he knew it was supernaturally achieved.

Dressed in white that shone like the rays of the sun, in a tiara of orange blossoms of shinning pearls, white patent leather shoes with matching white stockings YOU marched up the apse with her companions of The Holy Trinity Church. They looked like the wise virgins bearing the lamps of oil in their hands. This time, the lamps were candles.

The Holy angels marched with them. Only a few discerning Spirit filled souls were able to see the majesty of it all.

The organist played the song of the Blessed Virgin Mary as the cantor proclaimed in musical echo, the solo in rendition to the words of the hymn.

Heaven touched earth in preparation for the miracle of the changing of Blood and wine into the Body and Blood of Christ as the priest of I AM gave the blessing and promise to take eat and drink in memory of I AM. They were admonished to partake and to do it worthily.

The little virgins (boys and girls) would be breaking their fast with the communion bread and wine. The body was deprived of nutrition in preparation for purging of the flesh and finally for the infilling of body and spirit with I AM's supernatural anointing and transformation of a sinful body of flesh into the righteousness of I AM.

A miracle took place in each daughter and son of Zion, but none felt this remarkable change, as did YOU. Her face shone as the stars of heaven as the host touched her tongue. This transmutation of her body almost caused her to fall prostrate before the altar. Her guardian angels steadied her to her feet. YOU thanked her blessed stars of Heaven as she raised her eyes in praises to her Royal High Priest, the Father of Heaven and Earth.

A delightful Thanksgiving Dinner at home, with family and invited friends culminated the event. YOU gave an instrumental rendition of the Handel's Messiah as the closing offertory to I AM that I AM in her life of love joy and peace on Earth. You was a budding eleven year old, soon to be twelve and in the Sunshine of her years.

All rejoiced for YOU. The angels gave glory to I AM for the gift of life through the shedding of His Blood, Body, Soul and Divinity for YOU, and YOU and YOU.

Family prayer ended the celebration. Petitions were made for **those who were and are in most need of I AM's mercy and grace.**

It was time for rest and relaxation. With the usual blessings, everyone dispersed to their residence and rested in the Lord.

This was a day that the Lord hath made. They rejoiced and were glad in it. There would never be another like it.

YOU fell asleep as soon as her head rested on the pillow, knowing that her dreams would be like Paradise.

TE LUCIS ANTE TERMINUM

Creator of all things, before the close
of day, we earnestly beg Thee to be, with
Thy customary mercy, our Protector and Preserver
May our hearts dream of Thee and experience
Thee through sleep; and with a light near,
let them always celebrate Thy grace in song

Grant us help; keep us warm; and let Thy light
Illuminate the frightful darkness of the night

Grant these things Almighty Father, through
Jesus Christ our Lord,
Who reigns throughout eternity with Thee
and the Holy Spirit.

(From: The Adoremus Hymnal)

YOU IS PRESENTED WITH A HARP

Having been confirmed by the Priest and by the Holy Spirit, YOU was empowered by I AM to go into a three day-fasting with prayer and supplication to I AM for Divine Protection, Chastity, Healing Ministry, Devotion and Adoration by the Sacred Heart of Jesus to the Blessed Virgin Mary and the Eucharist.

She did as the Spirit ordered her and received the anointing of the Holy Spirit with the accompanying gifts of the interpretation of the Heavenly Language (Tongues) speaking in the Heavenly Language and the gift of Prophesy. These were immediately identified, but she exhibited other giftings as time moved on.

Instead of allowing pride to enter her heart, she became more reserved, prayerful and humble.

I AM instructed her to form a group of musicians for the band in her junior high and high school. She gathered all the students that were confirmed with her for a meeting.

They met, prayed and worshipped the Trinity after which she presented to them the purpose of the meeting as designed and instructed by I AM.

The topics were in a way conservative and Godly. They were asked to:

1. Make a pledge of virginity until marriage
2. Practice all the Rules and Commandments of I AM
3. Use their talents and gifts to inspire, give and serve the school and church family, community and country with self-sacrifice in the hope of conversion to Christ.

Twelve students and YOU signed up at the end of the meeting. Thirteen convicted souls. Someone made a jest of the number being of sad omen. YOU informed them that with Jesus there were thirteen in His company to start His ministry. She shared that after one of the apostle committed suicide, another replaced him. For some reason Jesus wanted twelve to be with Him. She **lightened** the discussion by saying "We are the baker's dozen. That's who we are. The Makers Dozen." Thus they named their group. "The Maker's Dozen" I AM is their Maker. They are His Dozen. With that settling the discussion faith having been rebuilt, they decided to work on the plan of action for their calling and purpose.

Of those that joined all were gifted in music, dance and voice. They all played instruments of music that were a requirement for a band.

They took their pledge of chastity and signed the contract associated with the pledge of virginity until marriage or until the Marriage Supper.

They practiced as often as they could and presented their band, their colour guard and music to the administration of the school and to the coaches of the football, basketball and baseball teams.

All were equally impressed, awed and at the same time delighted at the grandeur and professional delivery of the Maker's Dozen.

The school, Holy Trinity Christian School, accepted unanimously the gift that they offered. This was the start of a School Band for the school. They were not competitive with other bands. If they were they would be total winners. They played for their school and entertained the disabled and sick veterans, residents in nursing homes, children in hospitals for special illnesses and surgeries as time dictated and allowed. The results of the group's rendition always brought miraculous changes.

For as long as the band played for the schools, in practice or sports competition no one was injured or hurt in anyway. This finding was inspirational as it was mind-boggling.

YOU's parents were pleased with her accomplishments as the leader of the band as well as with her personal success and accomplishments in her instruments. They decided to present her with a harp.

Her sixteenth birthday arrived. Family and friends decided that she was coming of age and should be presented to society. This should be done at a Debutante's Ball.

Mind and hearts, souls and hands got together to plan the **Ball** on YOU's birthday as a celebration for life. The month October, the day the seventh, the time six p.m. until nine o'clock p.m.

It would be resplendent and resonant of a holy day, with prayers, praises, presents and the presence of I AM, His Spirit and Angels.

The Church Hall was decorated with tulips, lilies and magnolia all in white with the greenery of their beautiful leaves depicting purity and life. She was escorted by her Dad who would present her to her social associates and community of Saints from her parish and churches in the communities that sponsored other debutants.

The day arrived in brilliance and majesty. Holy Trinity's organist struck the triumphant note of the processional as the classical band and choir accompanied.

The debutants dressed in mint green gowns, white gloves, mint green shoes and with white corsages neatly displayed on their wrists, were escorted by their fathers as they entered the hall of the stunningly decorated room of Holy Trinity, to the rhythm of the angelic music.

In due time they were presented by name and district to all who were in attendance.

The most delightful and fairy-like waltzes were played as fathers danced with their daughters. The young Misses twirled and smiled at their beaus and their fathers who were presenting them to the world as the Bride of Christ will be presented to I AM on that Grand Wedding Feast of Revelation.

The dinner was blessed. The menu consisted of fish and poultry, baked Idaho potatoes, broccoli, garden salad, fruit compote and white non-alcoholic wine. All foods were, beautifully garnished with rose like petals of tomato peels, onion flowers, beet roses, watercress and escallions. The salad dressing was of a garden variety, the potato dressed with cloves and sour cream.

A strawberry shortcake decorated with blood red strawberries on white cake served on a plate lined with green magnolia leaves added excitement to the taste buds after a warm yet blandish and tasty entrée.

In the excitement, anything would be delicious, but the taste and flavour of a lovingly prepared banquet by the school's cafeteria staff was received with thankful hearts in greatest gratitude and devotion.

The speeches were grand, the recessional inspiring and uplifting, but the excelsis moment was the presentation of the birthday gift to YOU.

YOU desired nothing but love on her birthday. YOU felt that day should be dedicated to I AM and to her parents. Her church her school and her friends, knew that she would not be spoiled by a gift or any gift especially one that bespeaks and benefits her talent given by I AM. The gift was rolled into the podium where they dined. It was placed at the head of the table where YOU was seated. It seemed to be something that could envelop her (and so it did).

The beautiful wrapping of green and white was removed after a speech and presentation to a gifted, beautiful Godly and inspiring artist.

Oohs, Ahhs, and Wows erupted and disturbed the silence after the unwrapping, as a most beautifully carved stringed instrument appeared before the delighted eyes of all their owners, in the room or hall.

YOU accepted her gift with wonderment and surprise as she offered thanks to I AM, her family, friends and countrymen. The spontaneity of her remarks, belied her surprise, yet all knew that she had no, foreknowledge of a gift for she requested none.

As a part of her thanksgiving YOU moved graciously to the strings of her harp and strummed the Shepherd Psalm "The Lord is my Shepherd No Want Shall I Know."

Her guardian angels bowed in reverence to I AM falling prostrate on their faces as the attendees and debutants rose to their feet with arms raised in praises to I AM. YOU bowed her head with tears of love, honour and devotion pouring from her wounded, yet healed heart.

THE MIRACLE OF THE HARP AND ITS MUSICIAN

The grand mother of one of the debutants decided that despite her pain and affliction she would not miss this occasion. She suffered severely from crippling arthritis that rendered her immobile. She was confined to a wheel chair and had to be transported in this device by her family or social services attendant.

Upon entering the hall she felt the presence of the great I AM. She dedicated her life many years ago to the service of I AM. Many wondered why this "punishment" was on her. They would soon learn the answer.

The height of worship in this seemingly social event awakened a desire in YOU to dance before the Lord. "Why was she feeling this emotion," she asked herself. Her answer in her heart was "that the Spirit of the Lord was in this place."

Grandmother's body seemed to be getting electric shocks, as her lower limbs began to get warmer and warmer. This was so strange because her lower body always felt cold, especially her legs and feet.

As YOU began to play the harp all these feelings appeared. As she began to sing the words of the Psalm, "no want shall I know" feelings came into her now worn feet. The electric shocks jolted her to her feet. She was standing with the audience as they rose to their feet to offer praise to God for the gift of music and song that YOU had received. The harp was "stuff," but "necessary stuff." YOU anointed her "stuff" with her talent and a miracle occurred. Grandma left the wheelchair at the Church Hall and leaped home rejoicing. She was perfectly healed.

During her healing YOU felt a numbing pain in her heart. This happened before. This was her cue that someone was receiving a healing. That was a part of the reason for her tears. This would be her purpose for which I AM called her into this planet called Earth or World.

She gave thanks to I AM for His Call and for His gifts that He treasured upon her and upon the world in general. She thanked Him for the harp.

Her lips moved in prayer as she asked that all men would answer to the Divine Call of I AM in and on their lives and fulfil the purpose for which they are created.

In His presence there are pleasures forevermore. "Why does man act so irresponsible and nonchalant to the Call of I AM?" YOU thought. We are so seemingly carefree and nonchalant. Even when we commit we operate in a half-hearted, self-righteous way. Why doesn't everyone reciprocate the agape love of I AM, and give HIM the Praise, HE and only HE deserves.

CHAPTER 5

THE DEVINE CALLING

YOU AND I AM

YOU realized that there is a Divine calling on her life. In order to fully answer her Call, she must be in perfect submission to HIS will.

I AM fellowshipped with her in her personal walk and relationship with HIM. HE communicated with YOU in such a personal and almost human way, that some thought her to be demented. Were it not for her walk of obedience and faith, which was observed in the Divine healings that took place, life for her would have been a tragedy or travesty.

In order to stay focused on I AM and to hear HIS voice, YOU decided that there were certain precautions and instructions she should take and follow. Common sense sent her back to the manual on which she was raised.

She studied, worked, prayed, exercised, played and meditated.

A RULE TO REMEMBER

"All work and no play makes Jill a dull girl" she mused. She left her work and played with Siddie and decided to take Laddie on her ride on White Man.

The day was clear, yet balmy and full of music from the birds that nestled by her window in the lilac bush.

The peacock spread his plumage with beautiful array of colours and light as he cavorted and courted the peahen. All was wonderful in the world.

YOU continued her walk to the stable and she enjoyed the natural scenery of creation, and the Creator. I AM is **so wise and kind** she thought.

She arrived at the stable, saddled White Man as Laddie looked on in great anticipation for the run. Laddie loved this form of exercise for he thought he was faster than the beast.

YOU mounted graciously and carefully on the sidesaddle. She was aptly attired for the ride. White Man started with a canter, then a slow gallop and off he went with his tail raised to the sun, his ears as upright as an antenna, while Laddie pranced by his side trying to keep abreast with his pace.

Something shied White Man and he stepped into a hallow ground. He slowed down with a limp. Both horse and rider stopped, as YOU inspected the rear right leg of White Man. Laddie pranced around conscious that something was amiss.

White Man had a sprain in the tendon and YOU decided to walk him all the way home and back to the stable.

Dad had just arrived. He quickly changed, after observing the problem. He soon returned to join YOU and White Man for a first treatment to the leg. He placed vinegar on brown paper around the leg and carefully bandaged the leg, leaving YOU to pamper her steed into rest.

These sprains take time to heal. After supper YOU retired and prayed for a healing of her beloved White Man.

Upon waking the next morning, which was Saturday, she fended for Siddie and Laddie after checking in on her patient and stallion.

Into her room she went. She sat by the Crèche, made the sign of the Cross in a silent prayer for White Man.

She took out her guitar and began to play a love song to Jesus. At the sound of her voice, the Cardinals whistled, the peacock and the peahen seemed to waltz as the cat sat on the windowsill in total silence and enjoyment.

White Man arose. He began to stomp the rear right leg as if to extricate it from the bandages. Dad looked out to see what was happening. He went straight to the stallion as it continued to stomp as if giving a signal in music. He lifted White Man's leg. The bandages were almost off. The injury was gone. White Man was miraculously healed. He neighed and neighed and neighed as if he were giving thanks to YOU and to I AM. YOU felt the numb pain in her heart and knew exactly what had transpired. "I AM takes care of the beast of the field. How much more will HE take care of me?" thought YOU.

She continued to rejoice as her music enveloped her soul and delighted her friends about her. Dad pondered these happenings in total amazement and thanksgiving.

YOU visited White Man with Laddie tagging at her heels. Laddie jumped around White Man while YOU brushed his mane with strokes of love and praises to her one and only I AM.

News of the miraculous healing was noised abroad by the groom's man, who had been asked to keep still on the story. He could not hold his tongue. This was too great to be kept a secret; therefore YOU in order to escape the calls, left for a well-earned retreat for the summer break.

YOU AND HER MANUAL

I AM was blessing YOU and her family more than she thought she deserved. She decided to spend all her waking hours and free time studying the word of I AM. She wanted nothing more than to be in HIS perfect **will.**

YOU admitted that she was a sinner saved by grace and wanted to earn perfection. The Manual said, "Be ye perfect even as your FATHER is perfect." If there is any way she could gain perfection, she resolved to do so. The first was to study the Word, to show herself approved, rightly dividing the WORD of TRUTH.

I AM promised her that if she studied more and more, she would learn more and more from HIS SPIRIT. HE would give her the understanding she needed.

She needed not to be told twice. She obediently read HIS Word daily as the WORDS literally flowed off the pages into her understanding. She read the Bible, through and through, over and over again for as long as she lived.

Her memorizations of passages were extremely developed. Her interpretation of the WORD Spiritually endowed, as was her obedience to I AM's call and instruction for her purpose in life.

She grew to be sacrificially kind and generous, long-suffering, gentle, joyful, peaceful, full of goodness, forgiving, repentant and full of praise.

YOU'S PRAYER LIFE

The "Manual" told YOU to pray without ceasing and this she did as faithfully as she read and studied the WORD.

She prayed in every position imaginable, but her favourite postures were lying prostrate on the ground and kneeling beside her bed or before the Blessed Sacraments.

YOU sat for hours before the monstrance of the Holy Eucharist and adored her LORD until she was at times taken away in ecstasy as she saw her LORD on the Cross, bleeding from His wounds and crying out, "Father forgive them for they no not what they do."

At times she would see the Lord talking to the thief on the cross and saying, "Today, thou shall be with me in Paradise." All the visions would leave that dull ache in her heart, which led her to think the "WORDS", were for her and for her healing.

YOU prayed before the Blessed Virgin Mary. She asked Mary to help her to remain chaste and pure for her SPOUSE and for a husband, if I AM so willed.

She felt very close to the Mother of God and shared all her thoughts with her. Each time she talked with the Blessed Virgin she left knowing that all her desires were met.

YOU enjoyed praying before the Sacred Heart of Jesus and before the Crucifix. She was more than akin to HIM. Her heart ached for souls almost as HE did, and this endeared her heart to HIS. She prayed for lost souls, for friends and family, for animals and birds especially for her own "friends".

YOU prayed for the peace of Jerusalem for the Moslems, for Christians, atheists, agnostics, for those that never heard of I AM. She prayed for the rich and for the poor, for kings and for governments, for all the lands of the Earth that I AM has given mankind.

She prayed that man would love each other as her family loved each other and the animals in her home loved each other, their "masters and friends."

Love poured out of her soul for creation. She came out of her adoration and prayer refreshed, strong in the faith, in purity and in love, and in ecstasy.

During the times of adoration and prayer, she sensed and experienced her guardian angels as strongly as if they were living human beings.

Seldom would anyone impose on her prayer time or on her time of devotion. Her presence seemed sacred, and it was. These were consecrated times between YOU and I AM.

I AM filled her with HIS PRESENCE. HE anointed her with OIL. HE filled her with HIS HOLY SPIRIT. They communed as friend with friend. She was ecstatic with joy. YOU knew her every prayer was answered. Her MANUAL told her to ask and it shall be given, to seek and she would find, to knock and doors would open.

Freely she received and freely she gave. I AM loved YOU and answered her every call.

He was never too busy for her needs.

I AM admonished her, chastened her when she deserved and desired correction. YOU told I AM "Your rod of correction and your staff of direction comfort me."

She asked I AM to deal with her as HE willed but asked HIM not to leave her in sad displeasure.

In times of sorrow and mourning YOU experienced the Divine intercession of the Holy Spirit. As she groaned, the Holy Spirit groaned with her. She literally heard His groaning and felt His comfort. Her soul would swell with joy and very soon she would be on her knees again praying to I AM and thanking Him for Reparation.

YOU AND HER CONFESSIONALS

As Job presented himself before I AM in prayer and sacrifice, so did YOU lest she knowingly or unknowingly offended I AM. She searched her heart for any acts of disobedience that she might have committed. Sacrifice and blood offering I AM did not require. YOU realized that simple act of contrition in humility was all I AM required. Yet, she attended the weekly Confessional to present her guilt to the priest of the Lord. I AM required in the Manual that YOU confess her sins before men that she may be healed. What better man was there than the **priest and shepherd of the Lord?** She resolutely devoted this time for the purity and sanctification of her body, soul and spirit. I AM was very pleased with her integrity in these matters and as a result blessed and prospered her in all her desires.

YOU knew that her desires came from I AM, as HE willed them into her life. Therefore her desires were not hers but were and are HIS **will** in Heaven. These desires **must therefore be done on earth.**

What more can she possibly ask for? HE **was her Father. HE is her Father. She is HIS Child.**

I AM is the possessor of **her soul** for she has given her soul to HIM. HE is her Salvation for she has submitted her will to HIM. He is her friend from day to day. She smiled at the thought of the kinship between her and Abraham. Now she understood what it means to be ingrafted into the Abraham covenant.

CHAPTER 6

YOU'S MISSIONARY JOURNEYS

YOU ATTENDS THE CHARESMATIC RETREAT

The summer is upon her. Her prayer life is well ordered and orchestrated. Siddie, Laddie, White Man, peacock and peahen, the cardinals in the lilac brush are all in good stead. You have never wavered in her immaculate care of her friends and their environment. All the fowls and birds reproduced off springs. They were "free as a bird," to quote a phrase. The homestead was getting livelier and livelier as the playful birds and fowls exhibited their love and contentment in song and dance. YOU invariably joined in their praise with music and song. All hearts were merry. It was not unusual to see passers-by stopping to look at the **mascots** as they showed off their love for family and friends.

I AM coordinated and orchestrated the entire plan. Each family member and participant rejoiced in his way in praising and blessing I AM for calling them forth into this beautiful world of YOU.

The guardian angels that I AM assigned to YOU were always present. They could still be seen by YOU and by her pets. YOU's spiritual sensitivity was still attuned to the invisible realm. What seemed "invisible" to others was not invisible to YOU.

She was called into this world by her Father and Creator, I AM. As long as she remained faithful and obedient to I AM's call and commandment on her life the "veil" would be lifted from her spiritual eyes. She lived for I AM. She loved respected honoured and obeyed her parents and all who were in charge of directing the various areas, gifts, talents and instruction of her life.

As a result, she was loved and respected, encouraged and blessed. I AM opened doors for her as HE fulfilled her desires one by one by one. None of these acts spoiled her in anyway. She doted on HIS love as she did on the love of family and friends. She reciprocated the love that was given her and wondered why she was so blessed. Her only thought was to share her love in kindness and compassion, unconditionally to others. She was always mindful of I AM, as she prayed blessings on them and salvation for their souls; always being mindful of sin and being on guard against the enemy of man, Lucifer.

School had been most progressive and rewarding. Her grades were excellent the Maker's Band played for the graduation exercise at the school and was rewarded with a gift towards the expenses for the retreat at Long Branch Beach at the Catholic Retreat House, on the East Coast.

YOU's friend and member of the band chose to attend the Summer Retreat with her, in order to share the room with her. Each room was assigned to two persons. Both were compatible with each other, spiritually, socially and mentally. Their goals were almost identical and they were friends for as long as they could remember. They shared their hopes and desires, their joys and expectations. Their anxiety to attend the retreat was only outdone by their desire to experience the infilling of the Holy Spirit of **I AM** and to learn more of the plan of I AM for their young lives.

They prepared and packed carefully for the trip, making sure that their outfits reflected the coverings for which Father would be delighted to greet them as appropriately attired. They were always modest in their dress, no make up, no nail polish, no piercing as they were warned in the Scripture, not to make any markings on their bodies.

During their preparation time they fasted and prayed for direction, reparation and for the fullness of the Holy Spirit on the priest, nuns and leaders, as well as for the cleansing and purification of each attendee. They sought the Lord through the Scriptures and were delighted by the Word from I AM that HE would light the path and show them the way.

The day of departure arrived with great expectation, delight and anticipation as they readied themselves for the long ride. Their suitcases were packed. All was in place. Mom and Dad would be in attendance as well, and were the designated long distance drivers. They would not be drivers until their next birthday when they would take the driver's education course and be tested for their state's license for drivers.

Dad moved the car into the driveway. Joy spent the days before departure with YOU. They playfully raced each other to the car, laughing as they placed the luggage into the trunk. They told Dad and Mom to relax and allow them to do the loading since they had to drive for such a long distance. The parents of YOU acquiesced to their desire with humble bows of salutation.

YOU rushed back inside to say "Good-bye's to Laddie, Siddie and to the backyard to White Man. The animals were somewhat agitated as if they knew that somehow she would be gone for many days. YOU was saddened by her departure from them, yet joyful in anticipation of the blessings that awaited her.

Returning to the car, they delayed their departure for a few minutes of prayer for travelling mercies, not only for themselves but also for those on the road and all who would attend the retreat.

At the "AMEN." YOU opened her eyes to see her angels in escort as Dad **revved** the engine into drive. You blew a kiss to her messengers, smiled and totally relaxed her body in the rear seat next to her dear friend and "sister" Joy. The three-hour trip would seem very short, as the occupants enjoyed the scenery, sang, laughed, and pointed out the deer and other creatures they passed on the way. The highway was colourfully decorated with highway flowers, plants and trees. The ride seemed to be an unending botanical garden with butterflies, birds and insects. Fortunately, or as Divinely planned there was no road-kill for this would have put a damper on the young ones' hearts.

The moment of excelsior arrived as they entered the compound, parked and took a preview walk of site orientation. The young ladies exclaimed shouts of joy as they came upon the Marian garden of prayer. The Blessed Mother, beautifully carved and adorned stood with her arms open to greet YOU and her group and to "listen" to the words that most described their hearts at the moment of entrance. The garden was as picturesque as man could ever landscape. Despite the fact that they had to register for the retreat and be assigned rooms they decided to bless the Mother of God for her obedience in giving us our Salvation, Emanuel. With tear filled eyes of joy and solemnity they proceeded to the boardwalk by the edge of the sea, built about ten feet from sea level. No doubt this place was named **"Saint Mary of the Sea."**

The ambience and holy presence of the environment prepared their hearts for the long line they would now encounter, and the trek upstairs on the narrow halls to their assigned rooms.

After unpacking and refreshing themselves, they returned downstairs for the banquet, official service and welcome to the **"Charismatic Retreat At St Mary of the Sea."**

THE EXPERIENCE OF THE RETREAT

The Priests processed into the hall to the processional hymn played on the organ by none other than a Priest of I AM.

The processional was led by one carrying the Crucifix, followed by the Priest who carried the Monstrance with the Eucharist. Before the mass was over, there would be the Adoration of the Body of Christ after which the Body and Blood of Emanuel would be offered to the congregants as was written in YOU's Manual, the Holy Bible.

Each participant believed at the moment the Eucharist was presented to the words "The Body the Blood of Jesus" that he/she was eating the Body **and** Blood; **and not mere** Bread **and** wine, and accepted the statement with the same response, "AMEN" which means "So let it be."

With this faith all will be well; without this truth, many perish and are sick, because the repentance, forgiveness and reconciliation have not been fulfilled. No change has taken place in their hearts and they have accepted the Eucharist unworthily.

YOU shuddered at the thought of going before I AM without repentance while accepting Holy Communion, the Body and the Blood of Jesus unworthily. "What a gross disobedience and disrespect of I AM?" she thought. She shook her head as if to erase such a thought. She prayerfully asked for total cleansing of her body, soul and spirit and for the same of others.

> "Others Lord, yes others
> Let this my motto be
> Help me to live for others
> That I may live like Thee"

With this prayer on her lips in quiet un-noised song, she approached the Priest, accepted the Host on her tongue, after saying **The "AMEN."**

This experience offered YOU an **Epiphany** that she would never forget for as long as she lived. The memory of this Epiphany sanctified her entire being and bonded her Soul and Spirit to the total obedience and service to I AM for her entire life. Had I AM called her into Religious Life, she would have become a Nun, but I AM wanted her to walk among men as HE did, to be a Light and a Blessing to those in the dark world.

THE EPIPHANY

As the Eucharist was being served after the customary responses and prayers of consecration, the young children and adults customarily cross their arms across their breast as a sign to the Priest that they would not partake of the communion symbols.

It may be that they were not yet **confirmed** or that they had not gone to confession. The Priest then blesses them as he makes the Sign of the Cross upon them saying "I bless you in the name of the Father, of the Son and of the Holy Spirit."

Each person on approaching the Priest genuflects, gives the response "Amen" and accepts the host in the right hand, placed over the left, or on the tongue while standing, or kneeling before the Priest. He places the host on the tongue after the "Amen."

YOU was one of those who chose the kneeling position from which to receive her LORD's Body and Blood. As she knelt she folded her hands in the "Praying Hands" position, said an unconditional "AMEN" as the Priest intoned, "The Body of Christ" then the "Blood of Christ."

This was not the first time that YOU would accept Eucharistic gift of her LORD and SAVIOUR JESUS THE CHRIST. CHRIST means the ANOINTED ONE, "she thought. Before the thought entered YOU's mind, the anointing of the HOLY SPIRIT overflowed and overwhelmed her being. Simultaneously and instantaneously the host touched her tongue, she was enraptured in body, soul and spirit. She lit up as a Christmas Tree.

She experienced an epiphany that everyone was aware of. A light shone about her as it did from Moses of old, and as was recorded at the Transfiguration of JESUS.

From her humble position of bended knees, she seemed to rise from the floor, YOU's knees were still bent, her hands still folded in prayer as she was levitated almost above the Priest, who stood transfixed in awe as were every other congregant.

The only sound heard was the unison of "Ahhs," which proceeded from each individual voice at the exact moment. After **that** sound, there was complete silence as YOU's arms became outstretched in mid-air, while she floated to the ground in a prone position and in the form of the Crucified ONE.

Fortunately for the attendees, YOU was the last one on line to receive the Eucharist. How the Communion would have ended is anyone's guess. The Priest was lost in the ecstasy of the moment, which was quite acceptable in the intrinsic moment. No one has a true memory of the time-lapse and that is as it should be. In I AM time has no limit and no end.

The moment the Host or Eucharist was presented to YOU. The BLESSED VIRGIN MARY appeared to YOU, taking JESUS from the cross and presenting HIM to YOU. JESUS said, "Take eat, this is MY BODY that was broken for YOU, **so that your sins will be forgiven. By this act you will have everlasting life with ME.**

YOU saw the Blood stained Brows, the nail prints in HIS Hands and Feet, and the Blood flowing from HIS Side. Almost immediately the Body returned to the HOST or Eucharist with the Blessed Virgin presenting the Eucharist (Bread) to YOU.

Two mighty angels stood guard at Presentation and Transformation. The Blessed Virgin spoke to YOU and said, "YOU have been called to fulfil the Great Commission of MESSIAH. GO PREACH, SAVE, BAPTIZE, HEAL AS HE ASKS YOU TO DO. YOU shall do great things for I AM in his NAME. YOU shall bear the stigmata, but it shall not be seen. YOU already bear it in your heart. YOU will know the meaning of this very soon."

The angels lifted YOU to her feet. Everyone saw her propelled and wondered how she stood without raising herself up with her arms and feet. It was as if the wind blew her into an upright position from a prostrate landing.

The Priest and the celebrants as well as the communicants remained as dumb.

Soon the Priest begun to lay hands on his people, as one by one, each one fell, under the anointing until he at last fell. He knew as well as the others that GOD the GREAT I AM had done this.

YOU began to sing in the SPIRIT under the anointing, as the SPIRIT OF THE LORD filled the sanctuary.

Miracles happened as YOU sang, "The Presence of the LORD is in this Place."

YOU can feel His mighty power and HIS grace.

YOU can feel the brush of angel's wings. YOU see glory on each face. HIS glory fills this place.

Surely, the PRESENCE of the LORD is in this place.

YOU sang what she saw and felt, and all joined in with PRAISE, astonishment and THANKSGIVING.

The Charismatic Retreats would never be the same for those in attendance, nor for those who came after.

The HOLY SPIRIT made a determined and lasting impact. Every blessed soul made a complete and lasting covenant relationship with I AM that was never broken. YOU would soon be living her purpose for which she was called from BEFORE TIME.

THE THEME OF THE RETREAT AND WHAT IT MEANT FOR YOU

There is a time for everything under the sun!
There is a time to be born, a time to die
There is a time to laugh and a time to cry
There is a time to make merry and a time to mourn
There is a time to learn and a time to teach
There is a time for YOU to come into full fellowship
with her LORD and SAVOUR JESUS CHRIST
through the teachings of HIS Priests.

GOD, I AM, destined a Retreat for YOU, to experience HIS glory, an Epiphany through which her life and purpose would be eternally sealed by her convictions, through the teaching ministry, the Baptism into the

HOLY SPIRIT and through the wounds of CHRIST that she now bore despite the fact that they were hidden from the world.

Hidden from the world, but not from YOU, for she would endure the pain of the stigmata until the end of her days.

YOU needed to come face to face with her purpose. The Priests are well learned on the topic of WORKS, which was the theme of the Retreat.

Everyone would leave with his own experience of GRACE and knowledge that the protagonist of this story is YOU. YOU needed to be taught of the entire WORD of God as I AM HIMSELF inspired every WORD in HIS BOOK that YOU called her MANUAL.

I AM advised her that many believed portions of the WORD; but HE wanted the world to know that they should be obedient to every WORD.

For example, many believe that HE (JESUS) is the MESSIAH, and that HE is the SON of I AM, and as the SON of I AM. HE is GOD of the TRINITY. Since HE is GOD, then HIS MOTHER THE BLESSED VIRGIN MARY IS THE MOTHER OF GOD, which is not acclaimed by many. Many of the world's people tend to belittle HER significance, thinking of her as a sinner such as YOU and you and you.

This I AM pointed out as a misnomer. Another example that I AM gave to YOU is the fact that YOU is called as are others to rest on the LORD's day. How many actually obey this admonition.

As a result, many suffer fatigue, illness, disease, depression and oppression. The Priests of the Retreat discussed the third as their theme "WORKS".

WORKS

The WORD of I AM was given to the leaders of the Retreat the priests, just as it was given to YOU. YOU had to learn the MANUAL, the WORD of I AM in its entirely. She begun her reading of SCRIPTURE from the moment she learned to read. The HOLY SPIRIT was and is her TEACHER, even though AT THIS TIME He used HIS anointed Priests to teach YOU. YOU was cognisant of this fact at all times. Mother (Mom), Father (Dad) are also teachers, as are her instructors at school and church. She can learn from everyone including **nature,** but the HOLY SPIRIT is the TEACHER in all matters of truth and purity of the soul.

The SCRIPTURE readings:

> REVELATIONS 2:26 – "And he that overcometh and keepeth my works unto the end to him will I give power over nations."

> JAMES 2:26 – "For the body without the SPIRIT is dead, so faith without works is dead."

> HEBREWS 13:20-21 – "Now the GOD of peace, that brought again from the dead, our LORD JESUS that SHEPHERD of the sheep, through the blood of the everlasting covenant,
> make you perfect in every good work
> to do HIS will, working in you, that which
> is well pleasing in HIS sight
> through JESUS CHRIST; to whom be glory
> forever and ever.

> AMEN.

The Priests' Teaching on Works

Many believers do not accept the fact that **works** is necessary for gaining a place in heaven. As one really knows, we come to Salvation, through JESUS CHRIST and HIS shed Blood. By faith we believe, but **works** has been established for GOD's children from the **foundation of the WORLD.**

Works was established at creation and has been introduced in every book of the WORD OF GOD.

Faith and Works as discussed in "Wycliffe Bible Commentary" is described as the best known and most widely debated passage in the epistle (James 2:14-26). These were the verses more than any other, that caused

Martin Luther to describe this book as a "right strong epistle." Most of the difficulties in the interpretation of James 2:14-26 have arisen out of failure to understand that: (1) James was not reporting the Pauline doctrine of justification by faith, but rather a perversion of it. (2) Paul and James used the words "works" and "justification" in different senses.

James explains that only a false faith that does not issue in works and that is incapable of saving. By works James does not have in mind the Jewish doctrine of works as a means of salvation, but rather works of faith, the ethical outworking of true piety and especially the work of love. (of 2:8)

The concluding statement to the teaching of James 2:14-26 shows that the relationship between faith and works is as close as that between body and spirit. Life is the result of the union in both instances when the two elements are separated death results. "False faith is virtually a corpse" (FJ.A. Host; The Epistle of St. James, P. 45).

YOU researched the Scriptures on **WORKS**. YOU used the work sessions in her group to share her findings, from Genesis to Revelation. This was the deciding factor that her life would be lived working the **works** of I AM, serving HIM by **Faith.**

It was a miracle to YOU that the Priest's used **James 2:26** to teach the work of works, while her research ended at **Revelation 2:26.** "And he that overcometh and keepeth my works unto the end to him will I give power over the nations."

YOU gave the list of the findings, she chose to research, to her group. Each person was asked to finish the readings at home. Time did not allow discussions on all of the references that YOU would like you to review.

I.	1 Thessalonians	1:3
II.	2 Thessalonians	3:10
III.	2 Thessalonians	3:11
IV.	Titus	3:1
V.	1 Corinthians	3:1
VI.	Ephesians	4:11-12
VII.	Philippians	1:6
VIII.	Colossians	1:10
IX.	1 Timothy	3:1

X.	Hebrews	6:10
XI.	Hebrews	13-20: 21
XII.	James	2:26
XIII.	Revelations	2:26

You will be amazed at what you have learned from these few references from the Holy Book. What if you received all the references that YOU catalogued for her own knowledge and wisdom on works? Are you challenged: Enjoy the journey.

The remainder of the Retreat was as rewarding as the beginning. YOU sang in the choir organized on site for the Retreat. She played the piano in accompaniment as the anointing and healing of her body, soul and spirit continued. Her parents were exceptionally blessed, as was their marriage. They were astonished at the unconditional love that I AM, exhibited in all the lives of the participants.

No life would ever be the same. Each person left with a total commitment to be totally involved in sharing the Gospel of I AM to their world.

They left the Retreat with joyful hearts singing praises to I AM until they arrived safely and soundly at their physical abode called home.

All were greeted warmly by their pets, which missed them terribly. YOU's angels seemed happy to be back in a home that was resplendent of the joys in Heaven.

After a prayer of Thanksgiving, a delightful supper and sharing, they all retired to rest, if not sleep as they meditated on the event of the week's end Retreat of the mystery and love of I AM that everyone experienced. This was history.

The experiences of the Retreat left an indelible mark on the souls of the participants, and exceptionally so, on YOU.

YOU realised that the purpose of her life was totally and completely divinely led and inspired by I AM. Her commitment was totally dedicated in the service of I AM. There would be no looking back.

CHAPTER **6**

MISSION OF WORKS BY FAITH

YOU BEGINS Her Ministry of Works in Faith

YOU set her face like flint. She steered her ship forward in life, looking always forward to the Lighthouse that drew her towards the charted path of her life.

YOU had no doubt that; I AM, called her forth predicatively for His will to be done in her life on earth as HIS will is in Heaven. Her memory reflected almost minutely for weeks on end, upon the mystical events of the Retreat.

YOU conversed with I AM, sharing her every thought. She still communicated with her angels and was in subjection to her parents, pastor and all who have the rule over her.

The archenemy watched and waited to attack, but YOU had her hedge enclosed about her, and would leave no opening for him to enter.

YOU knew that her life would forever be dedicated to the service of I AM and although she would not enter a convent, she decided to study with the Roman Catholic Church in preparation for a life of chastity and devotion. She was enthralled by the lives of the Saints and studied them all.

YOU revisited the notes she copiously recorded on works, during her Retreat. She cross-referenced the Biblical Scriptures from Genesis to Revelation. She was thoroughly impressed with the works of Abraham in reference to his faith in offering Isaac to the Lord. Abraham became a friend of God. YOU noted that the Blessed Virgin Mary in saying, "Yes" to the Archangel Gabriel, joined her works with faith and this led to the redemption of man as in the case of Abraham.

All through the Scriptures, she read, recorded and realised that works was necessary to be as it were conjoined with faith. Revelations climaxed her total belief as she realized that we would be given rewards according to our works.

YOU thanked I AM for HIS teaching, HIS wisdom, and HIS love, as she knelt before her Crèche and gave I AM thanks, in fervent prayer for HIS call on her young life. She answered with a resounding "Yes! Lord". "Completely Yes!" "Lord Yes", "Lord Yes!" Tears of joy from the anointing of the Holy Spirit flooded her face, as she lay prostrate before I AM.

YOU studied hard during her high school years. She continued her music, her band leadership and her singing. She accomplished all her goals and graduated, summa-cum laude.

Many healings accompanied her music, her voice and her teachings. Her "fame" was spread abroad, yet no one knows of the suffering she endured with the unseen stigmata and the heart that still responded the needs of all the people she saw and met. YOU bore her cross without complaint, and I AM, kept her in HIS care as HE carried her, loved her and encouraged her. Her life was mystical. She spoke with I AM and with her angels as she did with her family, friends and acquaintances. She was every bit a spirit as she was a human.

Her relationship with I AM was as simple and true as it was with her friends. "This is how I AM wants us to be with HIM," she often remarked. GOD is Spirit and we who worship HIM, must worship HIM in Spirit and in Truth," she instructed.

YOU blossomed in love and devotion and equally so her cross and epiphany. JESUS, I AM and her angels revealed many prophetic mysteries to her, many of which she dared not share. She languished in their love and in the Unity of their devotion. YOU would emulate her creator to the end of her days.

College Years

YOU aspired in excellence to pursue all the education and qualifying degrees she considered necessary to prepare her for her calling.

She enjoyed her animal friends, her social and spiritual life to the fullest extent possible. She was loved and respected by her peers and professors. She travelled to Rome, to the sacred sites of her favourite Saints, as well as to Israel, upon her graduation from College and University.

There were qualified beaus vying for her hand in marriage, but YOU was married to Christ her Saviour.

No beau could be competitive in this area, and she mystically wore the band of Christ on her wedding finger. The circle that adorned her second finger of the left hand seemed like blood flowing in a circular motion. The ring of blood remained on her second finger of the left hand for all her earthly life.

Many wondered at this phenomenon. "These are the mysteries of I AM." YOU would share in response. When we walk with our FATHER, HE resides with us and manifests HIS love for us as HE did for HIS first Children, ADAM and EVE. I AM has not changed. You have changed. "When we walk with the LORD in the light of HIS WORD, what a glory HE sheds on our way! When we do HIS good will, HE abides with us still, and with all who will trust and obey!

College years sped with lightning speed. The Campus crusades were exciting, inspirational and transforming. The majority of students were converted from their sins. Those who did not profess salvation, walked in dignity and love. The warmth was too significant and breath taking to be ignored by even the unprofessed, as the Sprit of I AM moved on the Campus.

While other Campuses were experiencing some kind of unrest and disturbance, YOU's Campus was peaceful and serene. The atmosphere expressed divine presence.

I AM blessed the music ministry and the financial benefits exploded from benefactors that were spiritually and physically healed. The funds were invested for the WORK of the ministry to which I AM had called YOU and her twelve to fulfil.

A schedule of tours and concerts for her campuses was annually applied and the offerings provided an income for the group and for YOU. This gave her the liberty and the opportunity to travel without "script" wherever she went, and they were never in want. I AM supplied according to HIS riches in GLORY.

Neither the group nor YOU allowed "things," nor "stuff" to encumber their lives or their ministry. They lived simply yet comfortably, gave generously and proclaimed the Good News of Salvation, Restoration and Healing wherever they travelled. And I AM blessed, protected and guided them wherever they went, because she was true to her purpose and calling. What a magnificent child of I AM and what a magnanimous I AM. Praise be to HIS NAME.

YOU in the HOLY LAND

YOU was offered a trip to the Holy Land as a graduation gift after six years of college following high school. She earned degrees in philosophy, music and theology, in preparation for her ministry of WORKS.

She gratefully accepted the respite since she was beginning to feel the effects of study and hard work, curricular and extracurricular. Methodically and thankfully she prepared for her fall expedition.

This was not her first trip to Israel. She went on what was somewhat a whirlwind tour in concert, in support of bringing home Jews to their homeland. She longed to return to walk where I AM walked, and to experience HIS presence in a land that has been designated and blessed by HIM. YOU, a gentile was grafted into the tribe of Abraham, and was now a Jewess circumcised of the heart in JESUS'S NAME.

YOU felt her heart beat furtively within her as she prepared for the trip. This answer to her prayer would continue to reverberate in her heart until she returned home. The scars in her heart responded with its usual numbness of pain, and she knew that this would not only be a respite of a vacation, but that I AM was preparing her for a mission.

She spent time in devotion and meditation, conversing with the angels, the Blessed Virgin and most assuredly with the Divine Trinity of Heaven and Earth that called YOU forth for HIS pleasure and for HIS purpose. YOU was on excelsis cloud. She figuratively had to put weight in her apparel to keep her from floating away into I AM's presence. The anointing on her life was transferred to all who came into her presence to help, to bless and to pray. The awesome power and majesty of I AM was as present as YOU or I.

All preparation was carried out and all was in place for her "vacation of vocation." She felt and sensed in her spirit that this would be more of a vocation.

A Vision Before Her Departure

Dr. Kurman remained YOU's family physician and he monitored her carefully to ensure she was in good health for the exhaustive pilgrimage she outlined.

YOU was found to be in excellent health. The pain of the stigmata, the heart wound and the ring of blood left no deleterious effect on her physical well-being. These were her cross to bear spiritually and physically through pain and anguish, but not medically diagnosed nor curative. I AM gave her these marks of HIS and only HE could remove them.

All the pent up energies had been expended in preparation for the Holy Land expedition. Exhaustion set in over the body of YOU. Every nerve ached for rest and relaxation before the journey begun. She showered, brushing her hair in warm water that sprayed hurriedly from the powerful showerhead. Every spray stimulated her pore from head to toe. She emerged wrapped and draped in heavy fluffy towels on head and body. She looked like a sheep preparing to be shared by the Shearer. She had oiled, deodorized and perfumed her body. As she entered her room she was greeted by Siddie and Laddie who were now very aged, but their love was as young as the day YOU received each of them.

Her angels hovered silently desiring her due rest as they communicated their activity to I AM.

Exhaustion became sleep, which captured YOU as she fell into her comfortable bed that had never denied her of rest. Falling across her bed, YOU was instantly transported into the Land of Sleep where the arms of the Dream Catcher gathered her retired and relaxed soul into the mystery of I AM.

YOU rose through a cloud, that seemed to be the reflection of the fluffy white towels that wrapped her body, only she moved at a speed of light on the bough that was a rainbow. It transported her into the heavens. All at once she before the face of her SALVATION, JESUS THE CHRIST.

HE welcomed YOU into the Holy City. The City was lit with the Light of CHRIST HIMSELF. YOU observed that all children born or aborted were being taught by JESUS. They learned about GOD's plan of SALVATION and of HIS suffering and death for the **Remission of Sin.** There was a school for the Saints who died in Christ. This was the perfecting of their Souls. They must know as they are known. "They see as they are seen."

All thought, knowledge and places seem to be operating at the same time in the same immeasurable space.

The garden of heaven seemed to be in liquid colour of every hue that radiated with brilliance of purity, never seen on earth.

They appear to be watered by the Crystal Sea that flowed from the throne of God and was resplendent of its purity and love. YOU wanted to drink of the **Water,** and she was refreshed quicker than she thought of it. Her Soul swooned with the rapture of delight and love that permeated her being. YOU somehow knew that she would never thirst again.

The birds and the animals of Heaven were all in accord in unity as the lamb and the lion rested together by the Sea of Life. What a joy to behold! A child played with the lion and the sheep as they rested together as one. YOU at once felt the absence of her parents, as she wished that they were there with her to experience this **fullness of joy.**

The music of Heaven awakened her hearing to what seemed to have been there all along. She was so caught up, enraptured in the scenic beauty that she had not separated music from sight. Everything was in **unity** and enmeshed with each other. Now that her "hearing" was attuned to the sounds, she realized that music emanated from everything. The waters flowed with melody, the flowers breathed in song, the angels sung, the harpist played, the birds, everything. HEAVEN is music.

YOU thought of the Maker's Dozen. No music could they ever play that would produce such Holy and angelic tunes. She desired this anointing. She was in the presence of the Saints that she studied and loved so well. She called each one by name and of course so did they of her.

YOU felt at HOME. It was as if she was there before and had returned only without those she now knew on earth. Before YOU could miss them, JESUS and The SAINTS begun to engage her in conversation. She asked many questions which were answered before the words left her "mouth".

They were communicating **Spirit to Spirit.** No words were necessary to be said and neither feet nor transportation were necessary for movement. It was all of the WILL. Instantly YOU understood what was meant by "MY WILL be done on earth as it is in Heaven." YOU know that all she had to do to move her **works** and **purpose** was to will it on earth as it is in Heaven.

No one had yet spoken this to her, but the knowledge was riveted into her Spirit and she knew what would follow on earth.

I AM (JESUS of the TRINITY) told her that in Israel she would receive power to heal body, soul and spirit. She would raise the dead, but the greatest resurrection and healing would be of the Spirit, to bring those who are spiritually dead and sick to salvation.

At once, she saw herself on a street in Jerusalem. There is a lone woman in a crowd, blind and in need of love and a touch. You walked up to her. She was near the steps of the Church of the Nativity. "She touched the young woman's eyes and her eyes opened to the sign of the Cross." She could see. The miracle was secret. YOU told no one, but the woman rejoiced in her miracle of healing as her eyes shone as an opal. What a wonderment. What a manifestation of I AM's power and love! YOU was totally lost in the reality of the Presence of the Lord and in His majesty and will for HIS people. She knew that this healing had taken place/ or that it would. Her order was on the march.

The Community of Saints and her Lord, told her that no danger could approach her for the hedge of protection was completely secure about her that she could not escape, because her obedience to her call was magnanimous. She had worn the stigmata faithfully and without complaint. She was indeed the Bride of Christ. A ceremony was officiated in her honour and she was praised for her faith and love of I AM and placed in a white robe.

Finally, she was told that she would go back immediately and that all would be made known to her as she walked in the Footsteps of I AM in Israel. "Fear not, I will be with you always, even to the end of time," she was told. Many secrets were revealed to her that was unspeakable. Her life would speak for itself.

YOU awakened with a renewed sense of purpose and energy. She knew that only time could fathom and explain the vision, its meaning, and its fulfilment. Her family knew that a mystery had taken place. They were alerted to enter her room after her shower, to check upon her. She had been very tired and had promised to speak with them after the shower and shampoo. Having had not response from her, one by one they checked in to see what was happening.

They observed her to be in ecstasy, yet her body seemed to be lifeless. They watched and prayed quietly until "life" returned to her body. They did not panic, since YOU was known to be in those Spiritual trances on many occasions.

YOU shared what she could and everyone marvelled at the unconditional love of God for this child.

They spent the next half of an hour saying the Rosary together and fifteen minutes, praying the Divine Mercy.

All was well in the home of YOU, as they all blessed and praised I AM for HIS goodness and mercy that endure forever.

The remainder of the night was filled with restful undisturbed sleep. Each child of I AM awoke feeling refreshed as YOU readied herself for the trip to the airport that would end in Israel on El Al Airlines. There was no doubt that the long distance trip would seem insignificant to this young creature of I AM. She had enough to meditate on, pray on, hope on, anticipate and employ.

The miles were as inches, the hours as seconds as they landed on Holy Ground, YOU escorted by her earthly mother, her angels and the Divine Spirit of the Trinity. Their Presence were inexorably felt and appreciated and appropriately thanked and praised.

It was only fitting to enter into HIS gates with praise, upon entering the Land of Messiah. Unlike Christopher Columbus, upon landing in Jamaica, YOU decided to kiss the body and blood of Messiah, by visiting the closest Church to her hotel, and by partaking of the Eucharist.

Divinely ordained, there was a Holy Mass at the Roman Catholic Church and as "faith would have it," it was in English and Latin, two languages familiar to YOU and her MOM. How she wished that the whole family were there.

After the Homily, they accepted the Body and Blood of Messiah. Up until then, they had only thought of the Eucharist as the Body and Blood of Jesus. In the Holy Land, "Messiah" was substituted. It amazed them that they both used that name at the same time without thought. Was it that the Jews who were Messianic, knew Him as Messiah while those who still awaited HIS first appearance called HIM JESUS a Rabbi or Teacher.

The Mass was well attended. No one realized how well the response to the evening Mass was, until they exited the door after greeting the Priest at the door. Greetings were "Peace Be With You" or "Shalom."

As YOU entered the street amongst parishioners, guests and onlookers, she saw in the crowd, a lonely woman, seeking for someone. Some kindred spirits drew them to each other. The young woman immediately thanked her for her sight in the name of Messiah. YOU looked at her in amazement as they recognized each other.

She explained to YOU that she was there the previous night when YOU approached her touched her eyes, prayed for her and she received her sight.

YOU graciously accepted her thanks and vanished from the crowd, her MOM and guardian in toe.

These mystical moments were not unusual to her parent. Her mother understood. She kept all these mysteries and pondered them in her heart.

No spoken words were necessary. They silently gave honour, glory and praise to the I AM of their salvations.

YOU Walks in ISRAEL

When blindness is healed, it is not always just physical. All healings must be Spiritual. The Blind usually explains his/her understanding of an issue with this statement: "I see." Does he/she literally "see"? Yes! Spiritually, his or her understanding is more clearly and keenly understood, than the eye sees. If one sees with the eyes, is it literal? The answer is "Yes"! If one sees with the mind is it literal? "Yes".

An author poetically stated, "Love sees not with the eyes, but with the mind. Therefore is winged Cupid painted blind?" The healing mystery and the Gospel of the Word of GOD is always intended to be Spiritual even when physical. The greatest healing that man can therefore acquire is **one of the Spirit.** When this is effectual, the process of the knowledge of GOD will take place.

The only leper of the ten healed truly got the message of sight. He/she saw the truth of healing. Healing is the removal of sin – dis-ease. "When one is whole," Jesus said, **"Has no need of a physician."**

The Healing of the Blind opened YOU's eyes to YOU's own blindness. The LOVE of I AM was made predictably evident; HIS **Grace** unmeritable merited and HIS mercy unearnable earnable. The healed earned no favour by her actions or greatness. Compassion of a SAVIOUR, HIS GRACE and MERCY are the only Contributors to Healing. Sin is Choice. Healing is GRACE, unmerited favour.

All human beings believe that we have a right of passage, even to Heaven. Yes, we surely do, but not by any act that we have done to merit such a reward, other than by believing in the salvation plan of Messiah. We can never pay for this plan. It was completely paid for by Messiah. YOU understood this part of the mystery and vowed to be faithful to the Call of I AM on her life. Another **"scale"** was removed from her eyes. "Was this literal or physical or spiritual," "she thought. Her soul answered "All of the above!"

YOU knew that the carnal is intertwined with the spiritual. The body, the soul and the Spirit are triune as the Trinity.

One cannot be separated from the other in the LOVE of GOD, the CREATOR. Scripture states that the Body although made up of different members, these members function as one. So do the **body, soul** and **spirit** function as one. The body without the SPIRIT IS DEAD. I AM created MAN in HIS OWN IMAGE. GOD IS TRINITY.

The eye of YOU was as miraculously healed, as were the eyes of the young woman. It was as if she received prescription lenses to correct astigmatism. "There is a- stigma-tism of the soul," she observed. She bore the stigma-ta. This is a mark of MESSIAH's suffering. It is the mark of the SIN of man that the INCARNATE bore and took to HIS FATHER IN HEAVEN. ONE that HE will wear forever. YOU have been given this mark. She truly must bear the pain that accompanies this gift.

FIRST DAY IN ISRAEL

YOU awoke to life after a "sleep" that was as deep as death. The mulled the ideas given in Scripture of "sleep". "There is a sleep that is not unto death." "Behold he sleepeth."

She was happy to be alive, not only in body, but her soul and spirit were very much alive and ready for her trip to Bethlehem. Were it not for her mother (her chaperon) and the rigorous walk, YOU would have done the walks rather than the comfortable ride.

Although she was filled with "Shalom" her anxiety caused her pulse to beat and to rise. She would be in the place where Messiah was born. What a privilege, what a joy! What unmerited favour!

YOU experienced a sight that boggled her imagination. She was visually aware of every detail on the ground, in the sky and in the faces of everyone she encountered.

In Bethlehem she visited the Nativity, entering the site of the "place of birth" of Messiah. YOU found it difficult to understand if she were experiencing an epiphany or if her visions were real or dreams. One thing that YOU was certain of is that many of the children she saw in Heaven were those slain by Herod, during the first years of Messiah's Incarnation, for she met them in Jerusalem in their slain state, but resurrected and alive in Heaven. YOU and her MOM shed tears of joy for the Saving Grace of Messiah. They like St. John prayed for HIS quick return.

On their return to their transport back to the hotel, they approached a young man who was severely wounded and paraplegic from a bank explosion. Mother and daughter felt compassion for this young man. As they prayed YOU felt the response of her repaired heart and the pain of the stigmata she bore. She raised her hands over his head, not touching him, but in intercession asked I AM to intervene on his behalf. Immediately he was made whole. I AM has replacement parts in Heaven. Faith and obedience can bring them into use for those who need and call upon Him.

The miracle reminded YOU of the man at the **Gate Beautiful**. The young man Josef rejoiced and gave his life to his SALVATION. The "two angels" left almost invisibly as the crowd gathered. They wanted no notoriety, but gave glory to I AM, who is worthy of PRAISE.

Where was this path taking YOU? This was uppermost on their thoughts as they experienced the faithfulness of I AM to those who seek HIM and are then called according to HIS **purpose.**

DAY TWO – THE WAILING WALL

When one is joying in the LORD, time moves at Celestial speed. YOU remarked, "It seems that as my head hits the pillow, I am awake to a more glorious day than the day before. MOM, it is as if I am in a perpetual trance of eternal joy. Is this what is meant by "Heaven on Earth?

YOU's MOM agreed with her and shared with her beautiful daughter, that she experienced the same emotions.

They looked forward to this **day** with great anticipation of hope and joy. They enjoyed a beautiful morning devotion. No creature or creation can receive any measure of the glory and praise that belongs to I AM.

The creation knows to praise their Creator. YOU was more than grateful that she could come to the place where her Saviour was born and where HE walked. What a great privilege she thought.

It was rather timely to visit the Wailing Wall of the Historic City of the LORD. Both YOU and her mother decided to fast before going to the "Wall of Prayer." It is unusual for women to be there, but they would not impose upon the sanctity of this place.

They arrived at the appointed time and kept a good viewing distance from the Wall, yet close enough to observe and to hear the worshippers.

They had their petitions placed in the wall. They did not share their requests with anyone, or with each other. From the events of their morning-worship, it was not difficult to understand that their prayers were for the Peace of Jerusalem and for the conversion of the Jews to Messiah who already came and that they would join them both in praying for the soon return of the Son of I AM.

The sun had risen surreptitiously over Jerusalem, and left the morning with a vision of extraordinary beauty in the aura of light that shone over the city. The city was resplendent of virtue and grace that seem to emanate from creation to creature to structure to man. The warmth could be felt in their very hearts. The sun arose as if in honour of the CREATOR of heaven and earth.

As YOU stood looking at this magnificent city, she became aware of the awe that captivated Jerusalem, especially at this site of Prayer and Thanksgiving. YOU's guardian angels seemed to genuflect as if in obeisance to a spirit of power. YOU seemed more aware of the presence of the LORD being around, particularly since the "opening" of her spiritual eyes." Seeing her guardians genuflect, she quickly scanned the environment in order to observe the meaning or the reason for their action.

YOU touched her mother, in order to get her attention to the matter at hand. Her Mom had grown spiritually as had her Dad since the birth and surgery of YOU.

They were very humble and thankful for their gift of discernment, and were more than thankful that they knew someone was keeping guard over their daughter.

The scene around the "prayer wall" was spectacular to behold in the natural, but in the spiritual it was stupendous. Hovering over the Wall were gigantic angels and hosts of angels bearing swords and horns that look and sounded like the Shofar. They were on guard keeping away the demons of hell, and blowing the Shofar as if in readiness for war. The written prayer in the wall shone like spun gold, while the spoken or unspoken prayers ascended heavenwards like liquid mercury. The aroma of the prayers was as that of fresh rose petals. The giant archangels stood at attention across the wall, with swords drawn as if to dare any challenger that would oppose the gathering of the Saints.

YOU and her Mom understood the meaning of this army and felt safe for themselves and for Jerusalem. Their prayers as well as the prayers from the saints at the Wall and around the World were being answered. I AM has HIS angels guarding Jerusalem. No one needs to fear the enemy, just fear God who can cast the enemy and his followers into Sheol.

YOU arrived in the land of I AM and was blessed to understand that I AM is always in charge and that HE gives HIS angels charge concerning you, lest you dash your foot against a stone. If I AM keeps you from stubbing your toe, HE can watch over you in War and in Peace, in tribulation or in ease, in disease or in health. Greater is I AM in you than he that is in the World.

YOU and her Mom rejoiced in this thought and in the fact that Israel wins the war. For the remainder of the day, she talked with those she met, sharing the Gospel of Salvation and many believed. Her mission was on the move. YOU felt blessed to be alive and in HIS presence she enjoyed pleasures that would never cease. The evening Mass at the Holy Shrine culminated the evening. The two had forgotten to eat, so they ordered room service and went into spiritual oblivion only to be awakened by the alarm for Day III.

Day III – The River Jordan

Morning was spun out of the night, in which dreams of music dancing and praises filled their restful souls. They awoke to another beautiful day with the rising of the sun as the moon finished his course.

They refreshed their bodies with a shower and breakfast. Breakfast was light, somewhat Continental since they desired not to fast, but to take a small amount of nourishment to keep them strong for the walk and excursion to the River Jordan.

My, my, my, were their anxieties high. To walk the River Jordan where her Saviour walked, to feel the passion of John the Baptist as he forewarns of repentance, for the Kingdom of God is nigh.

To feel the waters of Jordan overflow her body as it did when John the Baptizer, baptized her Saviour. To "hear" the voice of I AM say, "This is my beloved SON in WHOM I am well pleased. "Hear Him." "Listen to HIM," "Listen to Him", "Listen to Him," echoed through YOU, in so strong a nature that it made her chill to her spine. "What does I AM want me to hear," she asked over and over and over. No answer being given, she surrendered her ears to listen and to obey whatever the call on her life was to be.

They arrived at the Jordan, with YOU in a daze as if daydreaming, but very much alert and in conversation with her mother and members of the group.

Both YOU and Mom wanted a Jordan baptism so the robes were ready for the aspirants to don themselves for this auspicious occasion.

It was a delight to see the long line of people dressed in white robes with scarves of white around their heads, as they headed to the brink of the River Jordan. One by one they gave a testimony of their salvation. One by one they were asked why baptism. As each one answered he/she was carefully plunged into the waters of Jordan.

As YOU watched those before her enter the flood of waters, she thought and pondered over the Naaman whom Elijah sent to dip in the Jordan seven times in order to be cured of leprosy (sin). The miracle was a Baptism to wash away his sin (leprosy) she thought. "This Jordan is mysterious. When Jesus was baptized he must have left a Balm in the water. He is the Balm of Gilead," she mused. Before she could finish her contemplation she was led into the River Jordan to be baptized. She went under and was released only to float away in the water. All were dumb-founded and thinking her dead, raced to her side. They pulled her in as they watched the expression on her face. She was angelic and the smile on YOU's face told that she was slain in the spirit.

She was awakened out of this "trance" just as Jesus, and the Blessed Virgin explained to her that her sins are forgiven and that her mission would be short for the LORD I AM, would be taking her home to be with HIM in so many years.

She was a bit shaken by these revelations, but somehow, YOU knew that her time on earth would be limited, but that she must fulfil her purpose here on earth. She wished that she had had a longer talk with the Blessed Virgin and HER SON, but that was His plan, not hers. She also knew that this was not the right time to share her vision with her MOM, who had also floated away on the Jordan River, having been slain by the Holy Spirit of I AM. After these two were baptized, others floated away also.

The Spirit of I AM was in that place and everyone felt it and knew beyond a shadow of doubt, that the Word of I AM is True and that I AM is the Truth and Life.

Day IV – The Via del a Rosa

YOU was beginning to feel fatigue, the one brought on by the anointing of the Holy Spirit. The anointing is too much on the flesh, but the Spirit rejoices in it. When Scripture says the "flesh is weak," but "the Spirit is willing," that is a part of what is meant. These Epiphanies, the hidden Stigmata, the Ring, the anointing upon YOU made her weak in body, but not in Spirit.

She retired early after a nourishing meal, hoping to regain some of her natural health for the coming day. Wisely she made that decision and her Mom agreed with her and complemented her on her decision. So off to bed they went after prayers and a few conversational exchanges.

Dr. Hyacinth B. Hue

The Day was bright with sunshine and in the sunshine of their hearts, as they awoke, stretched and begun to prepare for a light breakfast. Again, they felt like fasting for this trek. This day would bring more sadness and contemplation than any other. This is the day that was divinely orchestrated for them to walk in the footsteps of Our Salvation, Messiah, Christ, The Anointed one, Jesus our Lord!

As exhilarating as it was to anticipate this walk, it was on the other hand sorrowful and heart wrenching.

The group advanced to the starting point, the Garden of Gethsemane. Mom knew what it is like to pray expedient intercessory prayer.

Knowing that she learned this from the MASTER HIMSELF, her life flashed back to YOU's surgery and to the prayer and prayer-line that opened the heart of I AM WHO gave YOU a new heart (natural and spiritual).

YOU, herself was aware of intercession in prayer and the toll it puts on one's life. The SON of I AM is about to be crucified and HE asked the FATHER to let the cup pass if it were HIS will. They were so thankful that when they prayed to I AM for anything, it was HIS will and HE answered affirmatively. Yet, HIS OWN SON, because of YOU and you and me could not be excused for it was HIS will that the SON give HIS life for sinners such as we are. WHAT A FATHER! WHAT A SON!

Is I AM saying anything to YOU in that HIS SON prayed and sweated drops of blood without getting the answer HE asked for. Yes I AM who would not spare HIS OWN SON because of YOU, allowed HIM to DIE on SINNER'S DEATH, because HE Loves YOU so. YOU said that this was the greatest of all mysteries.

Although YOU was not allowed to enter the Garden, her guardian angels stood at attention facing the spot where Messiah prayed. YOU shed tears that came like heavy raindrops. She thought her heart would break. She was comforted by a voice speaking in her heart and saying," I did it all for you". She hugged herself as if to hug the voice in her heart, as she whispered, "Thank YOU LORD!"

The walk covered the place of flagellation, to the court, to the seven stations of the CROSS that led to Golgotha's Hill. This was the hardest walk that young YOU had ever ventured. Her soul was crying out "Stop"! I can't go on!" but her spirit said, "YOU must walk the walk." She bore the Stigmata and the pain was excruciating, yet only YOU knew what it was like, for no one could see it nor feel her pain.

She was most relieved when Simon came to the Cross to help in the transport up the steep hill, but the ache remained. Each Station of the Cross made his heart heavier and heavier, yet she continued with the other up the hill until they reach to mount of Crucifixion. She looked up at the Cross to find our SAVIOUR, but HE was not there.

They went to the tomb. It was empty too. Surely it was because HE was risen. All this time she could hear HIS sweet, sweet voice speaking from the WORD and encouraging her to run the race to the prize of Salvation. She was promised that she would hear "Well done, Good and faithful daughter, receive the prize that was prepared for YOU.

YOU fasted for the rest of the day. No food could entice her. She walked in the footsteps of MESSIAH and she suffered pain. The Stigmata became extremely red and her heart beat so fast, that she thought that it would come out of its place.

She rode home (to the hotel) in silence as they pondered the mysteries of I AM. The Messiah and Jesus the Christ Blessed Three in One.

YOU knew that her calling was in salvation of souls, healing of body and soul as well as comforting through music and song. What a responsibility this was, what a charge given to one so very young! What a generous and special gift this was in helping others through the unconditional love of I AM.

YOU prayed with her Mom, talked with her dad, enquired of her pets and family, showered and fell into bed exhausted and euphoric after the day of mystery and empowerment. The latter was her tranquilliser as she went off into a Land where only good reigns. Her dreams were of the mysterious day's events and the love of I AM.

DAY V - Sea of Galilee

The day presented itself as beautiful as ever. The sun was peeking through the curtains of her window, as if to say, "get up and be going, there is a lot more for YOU to see." YOU stretched, blew a kiss to the sun and rolled over to see if her roommate was awake. They were both being beckoned by the sun at the same moment. They exchanged greetings and rose to the fifth day of mysteries.

After devotion and a leisurely breakfast, they decided to muster the strength for this adventure. None knew what the Day would offer, but both knew that it would be spectacular and surprisingly enticing.

They arrived for the coach just in time to be seated and informed of the tour of the day. To the historic Sea of Galilee where JESUS and HIS disciples fished, spoke with crowds, fed thousands from almost nothing and walked on water.

The Sea is as beautiful as the Caribbean Sea, of blue waters as far as the eyes could see. The peace and calm that pervaded led every passenger with a deep sigh of awe and appreciation.

They thanked the driver as they disembarked, as if he owned this Paradise.

They had time to observe before getting on a boat to experience the ride, so they used this time to worship Messiah and to honour HIS mother by praying the Rosary. Throughout the journey, they were constantly reminded of HIS mother's role in HIS short life on Earth.

They were now in boats, seemingly built like the ones the Disciples used. YOU sat next to her Mom, holding her hands as if to communicate these feelings by the hands. They smiled at each other intimating that all was well.

The man at the helm spoke to them of the Biblical experiences that took place on the Sea of Galilee and on the land above the water. They were mesmerized by the scenery as well as by the description of the events of Messiah on the Sea.

YOU vicariously visited and observed what were described by their Captain. She could not decide what was real from what was historic. She was living and waking with Messiah as HE did two thousand years ago. She saw everything and everyone, and spoke to them as if they were friends in the past. "Could it be that I met them in Heaven," she said to herself. While she mused, someone asked her about the miracle she performed on the amputee. She smiled without answering. She literally covered her head with a scarf in order to be nondescript. Nevertheless, the questioning ceased as the guide again shared the history of Messiah to the tourists. No one felt like a tourist. Everyone felt connected to Galilee as if by a cord. The bond was Christian fellowship.

YOU felt as if she could walk on the sea, but thought it best not to try, but stay almost invisible. Rumours of her healing ability were rampant, she neither claimed nor wanted notoriety. Messiah was the source therefore all accolades should go to HIM.

She felt that this trip led her to feel Messiah in perfect form, physically, not figuratively. She swooned at the thought because she was wedded to HIM, especially so now. She had seen HIM as HE is and was.

This was the perfect day for a ceremony, so she made her vow to the ONE she always and would always love.

Truly she finally became the bride of Messiah and would worship HIM in spirit and in truth until the end of her days.

She rejoiced for the experience of blessings she received and knew in her heart that she loved Messiah beyond words and would follow HIM and fulfil HIS request on her life for as long as she lived.

Returning home would not be joyous but she would happily return home to Dad, Mom, her family, friends and faithful pets. The flight home was nondescript. Nevertheless, contemplation was high as both YOU and Mom tried to achieve some needed rest and sleep.

Forever emblazoned in their memory was each event of their historic and spiritual experiences some of which would be shared, others never.

Dad was contacted daily and was apprised of each experience; therefore he asked questions that could not be answered by telephone or by texted messages. He was so thrilled to be a part of their experience even vicariously. After most questions were answered they drove home from the airport in silence. I AM had visited HIS people and each of them was a part of it. They looked forward to the soon return of Messiah, where every eye will behold HIM in all HIS splendour and magnificence.

They truly broke their fast upon their arrival, with a haughty and nutritious meal, generously prepared and served by Grandma. Not only did she serve their meal but she supplied the anecdotes of all that happened while the two were away. Many of her stories included the pets who were anxiously awaiting their turn of hugs and kisses.

CHAPTER 7

YOU IN MINISTRY

YOU In Service

YOU was anxious to begin her work for I AM. She registered and served with Youth With A Mission (YWAM), for six months. During this period she was in obedience to the leaders working in various capacities as required. Her gifts were quieted so that she could concentrate on basic training skills that would prepare her for her CALL.

During this time they cruised to lands where the need was severe and the Word of I AM unknown. It was rather surprising to see how these citizens accepted their gifts and salvation through Messiah's blood. Their hearts were open to the Gospel and they received the truth with no prejudgement or argument.

On these journeys YOU led many to the Lord. They all felt something in her that was pure and lovely. They responded to her with love and kinship, feeling some spiritual attachment they could not understand or decipher. The grace of I AM was upon her and could be felt in her touch, her speech, her song, and in her dance in praises to her Lord. This was easily reciprocated by her students.

This young servant of I AM learned a lot from her experience and shared a lot. A personal testimony on the miracle of her heart led many to the Lord as they wept in joy for a Saviour and Deliverer that not only loved one but shared HIS love with all.

YOU found it difficult to leave YWAM but knew this was a temporary assignment to help in her development as a missionary evangelist. She received gifts from her pilgrimage but passed them on to her leaders for use in their ministry, only accepting a few shells and seeds. She would not be encumbered with earthly possessions for her ministry was unto the Lord, and not for earthly rewards.

Ministry in Jamaica, West Indies

YOU was contacted to join a group of health services team and ministers of religion to serve a community in central Jamaica; during a tent meeting of evangelism for the nation. The date would be pre-hurricane season, in order that there would be no destruction of the tent by wind and in order to ensure attendance. The services were aired abroad in an effort to glean as many attendees as possible from other parishes. To this end they were very successful.

YOU's team of musicians were made ready for the occasion with health team of medical and dental staff, nurses and care-givers, ministers of religion and their pastoral aides. Medicine, equipment and appliances were pre-delivered in order to prevent delay in service. At night there would be the scheduled meetings and baptisms and during the day, health and medical services would be provided through screenings and evaluations.

The group was sponsored by the Ministers' Fraternal of the Parish, by the Parish Council and by the custodes of the parishes. A large tent was raised in the form of an auditorium with a large platform and one thousand seats. By day the "auditorium" was sectioned off by service areas for counselling in nutrition, social services, and religious programs.

The Churches and their groups registered on the first day and were given respective tasks that would ensure the smooth and uninterrupted flow of meetings and services. Tent meetings take a lot of planning and organizing, there is even a requirement for watchmen at night to protect the equipment and furnishings. Financial costs are overwhelming and yet churches and evangelists engage in this mode of evangelization. One would be alarmed to know that people who will not enter a church may enter a tent while there are still others who will stand outside the tent even in the rain rather than seek comfort inside. We learn from experiences that in many cases the reasoning is that such individuals feel unworthy to enter a sacred sanctuary.

Erecting a tent requires experience and "elbow grease". It takes technique and strength. The platforms are heavy and costly. At times the platforms are the beds of a trailer truck. Chairs have to be arranged and a "watch" hired. The baptismal font has to be filled and cleaned and refilled each night for baptism of the new converts. At times the baptisms are held at the end of the week/s of Crusade.

The theme of the Crusade has to be discussed and developed by the Scripture – (chapter and verse) selected hymns, praise songs, choirs, speakers, leaders, ushers, hospitality, emergency techniques, lights (breakers and systems), programs and activities.

The same has to done for the daily activities, disposal of medical utensils (hazardous and safe), display of pamphlets, fliers, books etc. Fortunately the singers and leaders do not have to labour in setting up the intricate and arduous tasks unless emergency warrants their assistance. To deliver a sermon, to sing, and to conduct a choir and band, warrants a great energy which saps the strength from these workers.

Having arrived early for the planning session at the Retreat House, YOU made herself useful in assisting where she was needed. She very quickly won the love and admiration of the workers and staff who were willing to do anything she asked of them. Her spell of love was in operation. The anointing was all over her.

YOU left home on a one hour ride to the airport for a two-hour wait and check-in before her 8:00a.m., flight to Montego Bay. Excitedly she entered the Retreat bus to the interior of the island as she steadfastly gazed at the vegetation, the sea that frolicked around the north coast, the beautiful hotels, condominiums, and houses that graced the landscape. Every home had its own natural landscape and magnificent views.

As they exited the Princess Margaret Highway, the landscape changed. Now there were mountains and valleys and pastures with beautiful oxen that looked well-fed and healthy. There were goats and dogs that daringly challenged each motorist to hit them as they ran across the street barking at the motorists.

As the schools closed for the day the uniformed bodies of the students flooded the streets as if they were drone bees from a hive. Others suspected that there was a factory that produced these colourfully arrayed and neatly attired children. Every school had its own uniform of colours that identified its enrolment.

At the roadsides were displayed a variety of foods, fruits and vegetables. The most unique counter carried roasted yam and roasted salted cod fish as an accompaniment. The tongue and taste buds were delighted to have such a blend of exotic foods. The yellow yam hard yet tender and the salted fish sprung the salivary gland into a mouth- watering blend of joy and satiety. How could a meal so simply prepared be so fully enticing? Yet it was!

YOU arrived at the Retreat House in time for a tour and to assist in the preparation for the next day of activities. The driveway to the Retreat House was paved with concrete from the main road to the large gate that gave its name "Retreat House". The gate opened to a driveway which had on both sides, manicured lawns with a variety of flowers, fruit trees, cherry plants, sugarcane, miniature June-plums, and bananas. Upon entering the garage the party entered a well-furnished and polished five-bedroom house with four bathrooms, a large dining room that seats twelve comfortably, a large living room, laundry room, kitchen, store-room and a large veranda. The house was convent clean and peaceful. The Spirit of I AM was very present and desperately needed.

The second Retreat House was equally decorated and furnished with one bedroom less than the Retreat House I and the exception was that meals were prepared and served here. Retreat House II was about a quarter of a mile from Retreat House I, therefore those residing at Retreat House I got the opportunity to walk before and after meals. Retreat House III was a two storied building with the office, multipurpose hall, Samaritans House, postal agency and a medical, dental and health clinic staffed with a full time nurse. This facility was well furnished as were the other two buildings.

YOU was delighted to know that there was electricity for the buildings and for the tent, hot water for showers and for washing a washer and dryer for clothes and linen. She sampled the Jamaican cuisine at her new home after fully digesting the roadside treats of roasted yam and salted cod fish. She was fascinated by the flavours and aroma of the strange but delectable food. There was a hint of curry, turmeric and thyme with coconut milk in which slices of chicken breast were sautéed. "Rice and Beans" also was flavoured with coconut milk, pig's tail, garlic, thyme, and with Scotch Bonnet pepper. The smell was as good as the taste. YOU prayed that she would maintain her weight as she did in Israel. She felt the anointing and knew that it remained on her; therefore, food would be the least of her problems.

She visited the tent site and wondered if this seemingly small community could fill such a large tent. She assisted in the final preparation and set up of the chairs for the choir and for her band. The night choir would be that of the pastor of the church that gave the message and every night for the duration of the meetings.

She gathered her peers together for prayer after which they practiced a piece of the renditions they would offer, tonight. As they played, the anointing came fully upon them. They began to speak in an unknown tongue or language that flowed musically from their lips. There was an interpreter who proclaimed the messages that were spoken. "The revival would move like a wind that would cleanse the sin-sick hearts. The people will be given a gift that they will never forget. Jesus is our Salvation and must be honoured and praised. Repent and be baptized for the remission of your sins, thus sayeth the Lord."

The joy that flooded their hearts was more than they could embrace so they all fell in unison before the Lord as if slain. They remained on the ground for about five minutes after which each shared the messages that were imprinted on their hearts as they prostrated themselves before I AM.

People soon began to gather so they dashed off to be refreshed and to change into their choiristors garments. They were now as one in body, soul, and spirit and they knew that they were touched by I AM. The stories of their gift of healing had preceded them, and now it was known for sure that these are the children of I AM.

The keyboard struck a note as the guitarist twanged his strings, the drummer hit a sound and the horn tuned in with one melodious rhythm that resounded in the community to the tune of

> "Holy, Holy, Holy, Lord God Almighty,
> All Thy works shall praise Thy name
> on earth and sky and sea.
> Only Thou art holy.
> There is none beside Thee,
> Perfect in power, in love and purity"

The congregation got the fire and with one voice joined in the hymn of praise. YOU alternately played the keyboard, the guitar and the violin for the musical breaks between verses. The arrangements were stupendous. The homily each night was sanctified and faithfully accepted as converts came to the altar and submitted their lives to the LORD, with the resulting "Eunoch's Baptism".

The HOLY SPIRIT not only saved souls but saved lives through miraculous healing and anointing. Nothing would ever again be the same for the congregants and as citizens of these communities.

The LORD was not through with YOU and her team. Each would have a special encounter with I AM, but the following is the experience YOU gained and shared.

I AM Teaches YOU a New Lesson on Knowledge

YOU fell exhausted across the double bed that was topped with an "egg shell" mattress that provides comfort to its residents. She had time to only present her spirit into the safe-keeping of I AM, before falling into a trance like sleep.

Her body was extremely tired and it had to rest but her spirit needed to be refreshed and refilled by the mystical anointing of the HOLY SPIRIT of I AM. YOU found herself in a School of Knowledge with the teacher, the HOLY SPIRIT of the TRINITY.

YOU in her vision began to understand the imparting of wisdom, the reception of information and finally the understanding of the knowledge received. This seemed quite complicated at first, but by the HOLY SPIRIT everything was simplified.

The word of GOD is a mystery than can only be understood in faith through love. There are times when we receive answers to our questions but the information does not immediately become knowledge. That is, it does not immediately translate to information that you completely understand. The learning and knowing have not yet become one! YOU received information but it did not become knowledge until she was mature enough to accept it after searching for that understanding. By the help of the HOLY SPIRIT, YOU began to see with clarity the importance of knowledge. The knowledge and translation of 1st Corinthians Chapter

2 was "lifted off the page" spiritually as YOU realized what she was experiencing:

> That true knowledge comes through the HOLY SPIRIT. Paul states "my flesh and my preaching were not with enticing words of the wisdom of men, but in the power of GOD. How best we speak wisdom among them that are perfect, yet not the wisdom of the world nor of the princes of the world that come to naught, but we speak the wisdom of GOD ordained before the world into our glory".

> The wisdom of GOD was ordained before the World into our Glory.

> Therefore the wisdom of the world is imperfect.

> Knowledge is power when it is translated into an action that gets things done!

> Knowledge is the GODPARENT of all discoveries, explorations and inventions.

> Knowledge is awareness of knowing the what, why, when, where and how of anything. This is Power.

Knowledge is Power for GOD is KNOWLEDGE and ALL WISE. Hearing and knowing, unite to knowledge for the hearer. The hearer must hear with the heart as well as the mind; but these must unite with the SPIRIT of Man and GOD in order to be perfected in man. Thus man will receive knowledge and power for revelation and action.

I AM divinely explained to YOU that this knowledge that was before the world began was resident in the fruits of the Tree of Knowledge of Good and Evil. He quoted the Psalmist David who in wisdom declared "The HEAVENS declare the glory of GOD; and the firmament showeth his handiwork. (Psalm. 19:1).

Day unto day uttereth speech, and night unto night showeth knowledge (Psalm 19:2).

There is not speech nor language where their voice is not heard (Psalm 19:3).

YOU understood that man can gain knowledge of the CREATOR from the day, the night and the sun. Even its heat relays knowledge.

YOU, heard herself repeating the Psalm of David #139:

> "O LORD, thou has searched me and known me"
> "Thou, knowest my downsitting and mine uprising, thou understandest my thought afar off"
> "Thou compasseth my path and my lying down and are aquainted with all my ways"
> "For there is not a word in my tongue, but, lo O Lord thou knowest it altogether"
> "Thou has beset me behind and before, and laid thine hand upon me"
> "Such knowledge is too wonderful for me, it is high, I cannot attain unto it"
> "For thou has possessed my reins; thou hast covered me in my mother's womb"
> "I will praise thee; for I am fearfully and wonderfully made; marvellous are thy works; and that my soul knowest right well"

YOU continued to quote the Psalm of David unto the final verses:

> "Search me O GOD, and know my heart; try me and know my thoughts"
> "And see if there be any wicked way in me and lead me in the way everlasting."

The Divine Vision of I AM made YOU to see herself as she is known. YOU realized that she must now know I AM as HE knows her, for HE has hidden no knowledge from her. Knowledge not only is POWER as in MIGHT, but is strength. This is the strength that by wisdom we know that we have to endure all things even unto death. "Her one day or night with the LORD is as a thousand years". YOU was absorbing knowledge as if she were a dry sponge soaking up water.

YOU realized that I AM withheld no knowledge from her. She was able to receive as much as she was willing to take in. I AM would fill her "cup" to over flowing. HE is the GIVER of all that is good for HE is GOOD! HE is JOY! HE is FAITH! HE is LOVE!

As she awakened for the new day, her body felt as if it were a feather. She floated out of bed onto the floor, falling to her knees like a snowflake falling to the ground in the winter solstice. Her hands were gracefully raised, as if involuntarily to the air in a posture of penitence and praise. YOU knew that she must now acknowledge all her sins before I AM, seek repentance, reparation and forgiveness as she approached the Throne Room of GOD. She covered her head as if to be in sack-cloth and ashes as she prepared her heart for purity before addressing I AM.

Showering all her sins, cleansing her soul by the Blood of the Lamb of GOD, YOU began a song of praise that could only have been imputed from Heaven by the Holy Spirit of I AM. The words would be riveted in her body, soul and spirit, so that her memory would retain it for a new musical, resplendent of the Psalms of David.

She knew she could never be a David yet she understood from whence these inspirations of Divine Praises and Thanksgiving were down loaded into his spirit. This was happening to YOU.

She stayed on her knees in this posture of yielding for what seemed like minutes; but they were actually hours. She floated to her music sheets and to her harp where she recorded, sang and played the Song of Joy: that was birthed in her. This song would be instrumental in the healing and salvation of many.

I AM showed YOU certain facts about the Sinner.

> Guilt: The loss of integrity of Soul. (The soul recognizes that fact).
> Unhealthy Guilt: The guilt that leads to despair.
>
> Penitence: GOD cannot resist a penitent heart.

Forgiveness: Brings healing and GOD's forgiveness.

Repentance: Produces love and Healing.

Confession: The Healing of Body, Soul and Mind.

Love: Everlasting; comes from GOD and through GOD and by GOD in the redemption of HIS SON.

YOU now began to prepare her "house" for her "home going". She instinctively knew that her life on earth would soon be over but that her "life" was eternal or everlasting. The Holy Spirit was imputing wisdom and knowledge in her as her eyes became clearer for her vision into life here-after. She had no fear of death "Fear of Death is absence from the Lord". The Lord was present within her therefore she was present in HIM. She whispered the Psalm of David. "Take not Thy Holy Spirit from me." As she did, she realized instantaneously what Death is, absence from the Spirit of I AM.

YOU rejoiced at the thought that "death is swallowed up in victory. O death where is thy sting."

> Oh grave thy victory
> The LORD has conquered hosts of sin to set the captives free.
> HE suffered grief and agony
> HE gave HIS precious Life.
> So great the debt of sin, no power on earth could save,
> No mortal life was pure enough to set the captives free,
> But JESUS came on earth, in bonds of sin and shame,
> HE suffered grief and agony,
> HE gave HIS precious life!
> All glory to HIS name!
>
> (Author Unknown)

With contrition, confession, and true penitence before I AM, YOU received forgiveness and Divine approbation from I AM: to continue her service in the HIS "Army".

YOU now understood "Resurrection". This Baptism in the NAME of I AM gave her a sense of Resurrection that she never understood before. "Knowledge is strength" she now knew. Experience is "Knowledge". She was Divinely resurrected through the Baptism in the Blood of Jesus and was now resurrected into Everlasting Life with I AM.

"What a fellowship"

"What a joy Divine"

"Basking in the Sea of Forgetfulness"

"Freeing her soul of Sin"

"And Rising to Heights before, Unknown"

"Free! Free! At Last!"

YOU would teach these truths to the end of her days. She would live these truths to her dying day. She would love and serve I AM eternally. Thus her troth was said and made. She was now extremely betrothed to I AM.

Sadly the pain on the ring finger and in her heart was as grave as her love for I AM. No cross, no crown, she thought. "My LOVE," she whispered as if speaking to someone she saw "I will bear your cross with YOU until I am with You. My strength comes from You, LOVER of my soul!"

The hidden wounds made her body weak and her soul strong: yet she quietly and prayerfully arose to complete here daily ministrations, which were her "reasonable service".

Once again YOU came to minister and was ministered to, realizing that one cannot out give the Lord.

The Revival, the Salvations, the Healings, the Baptisms, The Outpouring of the Holy Spirit flowed supernaturally. The entire experience was perfect as only I AM can do. This chapter would be over, but the pages could never be closed as YOU and her Team returned to their homes from flying from one country to the other by airplane; but had flown home from this mission, by the Spirit of I AM.

YOU Goes into a Retreat of Seclusion with I AM

The family of YOU, the dear pets she loved as dearly as they loved her, her faithful priests, her caring teachers, the friends, the neighbours and even her faithful ministering angels, were just a part of I AM's plan for the nurturing and admonition of YOU's life. They were all one component to frame and mold YOU into the one whom I AM wanted her to be. The truly most important thing is her birth was and is YOU's personal relationship with GOD.

YOU knew this instinctively and spiritually by her "training" at home and at Church that I AM wanted to be personally conjoined to her and she was to HIM alone. She had been loaned to her parents and to us while her life existed on this planet.

YOU loved, obeyed, and administered to her parents, her Church, her neighbours far and near. YOU never rebuffed nor ignored the angels that ministered to her for her entire life on earth. They were a part of her life as were her family and friends. They had protected her from danger on many occasions, for which YOU thanked and praised I AM for their presence and for HIS Goodness, Mercy and Grace. You never worshipped her angels. Her worship was and is for Jehovah I AM.

YOU never complained of nor dwelt upon her disappointments, pain nor losses. "Every disappointment is God's appointment," she would explain. I AM brought every sorrow in her life into a treasure of faith and goodness. YOU bore every cross as a heart with never a complaint before I AM. YOU was truly called "a child of GOD".

Miraculously, YOU's pets lived as long as she did. She was blessed coming in and going out. Her parents and grand-parents, her priests and friends all lived to the end of YOU's days on earth.

YOU's Knowledge of Life

The pain YOU suffered from her hidden stigmata of heart and "ring" finger seemed to be most excruciating at nights.

Night was created for rest. When evil entered the WORLD in the "temptation of Eve the Mother of All Flesh" the fallen, Lucifer embraced the darkness called "night" as a cover for evil. Thus pain and sorrow seem more severe, and is in the quiet "lonely" hours of the night. Loneliness is a misnomer of night, since I AM gives us a song in the night. In the darkest of the hours of the night I AM is there. His light comes in from the stars of the planets of space.

The stars shine through to bring HIS light into the darkest hours as if to erase all that is evil. The falling star reminds YOU of HIS LIGHT of LOVE. Many acquaint the full moon with evil, but the full moon brings light to reveal the evil that grows in darkness.

This light rebukes the evil by displaying I AM's light reflecting from the moon. The evil howls and moans because he is afraid of the LIGHT of the WORLD the SON of I AM. He is blinded by the light of purity and love.

As YOU bows before the Cross, with Rosary in hand the pain is multiplied in the darkness. The darkest hours pass and her room is bathed in the LIGHT of the silvery moon as relief floods her soul. Soon morning would break. The full sunshine of the Sonship of I AM breaks from the East and floods the room with light, as if Jesus the LIGHT of the WORLD has appeared to wash away the sin of pain and bathe her in the LIGHT of beauty and grace as only I AM can offer.

Her Place of Retreat

As often as YOU was able she departed to the brow of a hill next to her home, but far away from human sight to be in communion with I AM. Here she prayed, asked for forgiveness, made reparations, offered intentions, and received directions from I AM concerning her purpose. YOU prayed the Chaplet of Divine Mercy, the Rosary, and sang hymns of praise and thanksgiving. She read the day's Scripture. Should it rain, she went to the Chapel and spent this time before the Monstrance of the Holy Sacrament.

Each time she presented herself before the Lord she recommitted and was filled by the power of I AM's Holy Spirit, who inhabited her life. I AM was well pleased with YOU. YOU loved I AM. YOU loved her parents and relatives. YOU loved her Church. YOU loved her angels. YOU loved her pets. YOU loved her music. Yet her love had not diminished, should she have enemies, she loved them too. Her love had multiplied as she found new souls to love.

YOU reached out in her young years to find an orphan to love and to support. She "adopted" an orphan through the Church and supported her "daughter" from infancy. Updates on her "daughter's" life added to telephone and written conversations from her, enriched her love as she experienced the grace given to her by I AM to embrace a child though not genetically. YOU would ensure that her "daughter" was taken care of until she reached independence in age and responsibility. Her education was fully funded. Her future would be secured in the hands of I AM. I AM confirmed this, thereby giving them both peace of mind.

YOU's Blessings!

The earnings from the music of YOU and her musicians gave them great prosperity. Other gifts and offerings were donated to the organizations that sponsored her musical team. YOU kept the most personal items such as soaps, scarves and perfume. However, even these in excesses were given away to those in need.

YOU ensured that her parents would not suffer from financial distress. By the help of I AM, she prepared a trust from her income and royalty to ensure a buffer, if the need arose. Sufficient income would be there to take care of her darling creatures. YOU's plan of action was discussed and understood by her parents and clergy. She was following her life's purpose as directed by I AM.

During her years of travel, YOU visited as many Holy sites as she could, particularly those sites where the Madonna appeared. She was a pilgrim to Lourdes, Medjugorje, Mexico (Guadalupe), Japan and Knock.

YOU studied the lives of the Saints, Martyrs, Popes and Bishops. She read all she could on the great apologetics in history, and was totally convinced of the road that would be now her path, as she held onto only one item of her possessions, her harp. She needed no script nor purse and no clothing save the bare necessities and a burlap robe or gown.

I AM prepared YOU to be an intercessor for all, but most importantly for those who are in most need of I AM's mercy. During this period of preparation YOU fasted and prayed for extended periods of time. She often departed to her hillside retreat for contemplation. I AM revealed to her HIS absolute plan for her life. She consecrated her life entirely to HIS service and direction as she readied for her new path as paved by I AM.

The Parents of YOU

The admirable parents of YOU, rejoiced daily for this opportunity appointed them to be the ward of YOU. They could have been childless had they not prayed for a miracle. The infant could have returned to I AM at age three months. That could have been a blessing to have experienced the birth of so lovely a child, she was a loan.

YOU's parents long knew that this was a great grace given in the form of a privilege to raise I AM's "child". They performed this task as one of love. They administered their roles as parents as if they were raising the Holy Infant. Their every thought was to fulfil this awesome responsibility as if the "unseen eyes" were on them and know that this innocent infant's life forever depended on their efforts of love, truth, righteousness and the Commandments of God.

They studied the manual I AM had given them in preparation for "Raising YOU". They would follow it to the letter. The "theme" of the "Manual" to them was and is:

"Train up a child in the way he should go and when he is old, he will not depart from it."

(The Godly parents replaced the "he" with "YOU").

"Train up a child in the way YOU should go and when YOU is old, she will not depart from it."

They concluded that they had done the best they could. Even YOU's angels could not have done better. Despite the troubling thoughts that they may not have made the right judgement call in each situation I AM confirmed in their spirits, that they had done well. "The enemy will always plant doubt in our thoughts" they concluded, "but we must never allow doubt to be entertained." I AM does all things well! The family's hope and faith were in "excelsis Deo".

To say that they were not concerned and thoughtful about YOU's decision and her future would be false; but once they had put their trust in I AM, their faith had no limit.

CHAPTER **8**

YOU DEPARTS

YOU's Preparation

You started packing for months before the scheduled time, although the few items she selected (not including her harp) could be held in a "backpack". She carefully labelled items that were passed on for personal gifts, donations to organizations, memorabilia to her church and museum and for grab bags to the children of the community. YOU researched and visited Religious Communities that spent their time in intercession, contemplation, reparation, fasting, and worship. Parents and child felt the sadness of the coming movement, especially when YOU packaged her religious icons as part of her effects. They were held together in these critical times, by "glue" called "trust and obedience". They all knew that "trust" is the link to the son of I AM; and that "obedience" has been the key to true worship of I AM, since the World Began in Eden. "Obedience is better than sacrifice", they quoted on a regular basis. "Of whom much is forgiven much is required"

During troubled times one can hear the family singing (unbeknownst to each other):

> "When we walk with the LORD,
> In the light of HIS WORD,
> What a glory HE sheds on our way!
> When we do HIS goodwill
> HE abides with us still;
> And to all who will trust and obey,

> Trust and Obey, for there is no other way
> To be happy in JESUS,
> But to Trust and Obey

YOU said her fond and yet sad "Good-byes" to each and every one. She refused the offer of a farewell party. The strain on every heart would have been ethereal. The Priest and Church family, Community and citizens, YOU's paediatrician and the medical team chose a specially arranged time and schedule to bid adieu to YOU. Hearts teared, eyes refused to weep as each soul expressed their love and fond wishes. All were careful not to mention nor reflect on emotional experiences of love and affection. These would sadden their hearts and change the festive occasion they encouraged.

Bouquets of flowers, balloons and posters showed the expression of love and devotion that blessed the congregants. The music resounded in soft rendition symbolic with the choir of Heaven. Love flowed as did the Precious Blood of YOU's Saviour on Calvary. The HOLY SPIRIT could be felt as warm oil coursing through and over the body inspiring, justifying, glorifying and blessing each and every one as they were all in one accord.

YOU's guardian angels attentively watched over the proceedings as protectively and lovingly as they did from her birth. I AM looked down with HIS unconditional love and blessed the joyous yet sad festivity. Hugs, kisses and blessings were exchanged as the guests processed into the evening. YOU would leave at the birth of morn.

YOU Departs

The household stirred at the break of dawn. All seemed as quiet as the grave as they moved about unbeknownst to each other in preparation for a quick breakfast; prayer for God's speed and the arrival of the carriage that would take Blessed YOU on her route to her "final destination".

YOU was always leaving for one assignment or the other. This should have been as the usual departures. But, no! Each one felt as if he would see her in this life no more. All wore a veil of hope and joy, not allowing the other to see the fire of love and sadness that burned in their very soul. She had been a star of hope and love in their midst, and they in hers. I AM had prepared this community and family of saints to raise YOU in HIS admonition. She had been the most obedient and loving child. I AM was well pleased with her. YOU avoided sin as if it were a plague and it is.

> Solomon says in Ecclesiastes 8:11,
> "Because the sentence against
> an evil work is not executed
> speedily, therefore the sons
> of men is fully set in them
> to do evil."

YOU feared evil and shunned the very appearance of evil. As a result, I AM protected her and gave her the desires of her heart. It was her final desire to spend the rest of her life on earth in prayer and supplication for the dying souls of men.

No fond farewell, no words needed to be said. Pure and undefiled love poured out from each heart as each caressed the other while the "oil of anointing poured warmly over their frozen being". "How can one be freezing and warm at the same time?" they thought; yet they knew that this is the Mystery of I AM.

Breakfast was simple but well received. This would be their last meal together at home.

Prayer for guidance, direction, and hope was offered by her favourite Priest, who offered the final Eucharist to his beloved daughter; for this would never be given her again in her own home or in her own town. As YOU received the Body of Christ on her tongue, the hidden stigmata within her body ached with passion for her LORD and for her call to final duty.

As the final blessing was offered YOU moved graciously and lovingly and obediently to answer her Call, as her family, friends, and Priest of the Church, led her to the waiting carriage.

Her head held high, her heart bowed low, YOU departed on her one-way mission to The Holy Mother of Jesus Retreat for the Religious, offering herself to her MAKER, to bear HIS cross for the intercession of SOULS.

The Arrival

After a long and tedious travel, YOU arrived at her chosen Retreat. She was greeted warmly, yet simply with no fanfare. She expected none. "All Praise and Glory were and are due only to I AM" she mused.

The Religious sisters closed the door to the world as YOU knew it. She was led to her small room, where she was divested of last possession her clothing, and robed in the simplest of burlap vestment covering her virgin body from head to toe. Sandals were placed on her feet and the final marriage to I AM was officiated as a simple gold ring was placed on her ring finger. The ring was absorbed into the miraculous ring she wore! A ring of light emanated from her finger.

YOU accepted her marriage to her spouse and went into ecstasy, as I AM in the IMAGE of JESUS of NAZARETH, reached out HIS HAND to accept HIS BRIDE. The moment HIS nailed, pierced hands touched her stigma, YOU's life floated into the ARMS of I AM. Her angels and her LORD with HIS MOTHER at HIS side bore her into eternity, as she murmured her final words:

"HOME at LAST and FOREVER with I AM".

Dr. Hyacinth Simmonds Hue was born in Tweedside, Clarendon. She attended Tweedside Elementary School until age 10, when her grandmother and aunt took her to May Pen, as she continued her Elementary education and passed the first Jamaica Local examinations. Mr. Walter King became the principal of Maryland Elementary School and the family moved to Maryland where she sat for her second Jamaica Local examinations. She returned to Tweedside at age 13 to take the third Jamaica Local examinations . After being laid off she had a stint at the Ministry of Labour. From there she applied to the Ministry of Education for permission to study abroad. In this she was successful and on January 17th, 1957 (two weeks late of the semester) she arrived at Tuskegee Institute (Tuskegee University) where she claimed all the scholastic awards; national, academic and Institute. She graduated Magma Cum Laude and was awarded a fellowship in order to continue the Master's Degree. Later she accomplished her PhD Nutrition and Doctor of Christian Psychological Counseling (DPCP). She retired from New York State Education Department Division of Finance and Management as Associate Chief of Nutrition and Finance Management. Dr. Hue is a registered Nutritionist/Dietitian in the state of New York.

Before the State, she was Nutrition Director of Project Head Start (City of New York) where she pioneered several programs and was granted a large fund for a proposal she wrote for the first Breakfast Program which has been extended through the United States and its protectorate, in the public and private (Elementary and Secondary) schools.

Since her utterance in childhood, Dr. Hue has had the willingness to care for children, the elderly and the needy.

She met and married her love, the man she asked of the Lord and they are the proud parents of 8 Godly children, 23 grandchildren and four great-grandchildren.

The miracles in her life are many and daily. One of which is God telling her to purchase the old school land. She did. Years later God told her to build a Retreat House for burnt out pastors, evangelists and missionaries, stating that they will help the people as they retreat and recoup their strength.

Without any help other than her children, she built Zoe Retreat, renovated her parent's home as Retreat #2, renovated Rev. Desmond Thompson's family home as Zoe Retreat #3 for a Boy's Home. Then she was told of a vision by Mrs. Desmond Thompson of a two storied building on the Shaw's property which is what is seen there today.

She has been all things to all people, from education to community church and members, to schools and institutions, to hospitals and government. Her vocation to help children and to give is untiring. She built and furnished a one room house for a citizen whose residence was destroyed by time and weather, and constructed indoor bathrooms for two elderly citizens. She paid for education for many students in high school and colleges.

She continues to feed the hungry and to minister to the body, soul and spirit. She ministered in the Tweedside Church of God Jamaica for many years. She is a scheduled Minister of the Frankfield Baptist Circuit of Churches. (Formerly 6 churches now divided to 3). She has ministered in Great Britain, USA and is a Bishop.

Printed in the United States
By Bookmasters